Meaning It

I0619002

Anne O'Gleadra

Beaten Track
www.beatentrackpublishing.com

Meaning It

First published 2018 by Beaten Track Publishing
Copyright © 2018 Anne O'Gleadra

All rights reserved.

Paperback ISBN: 978 1 78645 140 8

Cover Design: Roe Horvat

Beaten Track Publishing,
Burscough, Lancashire.
www.beatentrackpublishing.com

Nineteen years old. Divorced. Famous. In love with his best friend. Not exactly how Benjamin thought his life would play out.

Benjamin has known Dagen Mercutio (real name) since elementary school. Together, they're one half of a successful emo band where Dagen exploits the chemistry between them for profit. But being crammed into a tiny tour bus with a notorious heartbreaker isn't as fun as it sounds. As things heat up between them, Benjamin has to decide whether to walk away—or to risk it all for love.

From the writer of *It's Like This* comes a new story about sex, love, and pop punk in the early 00s.

Meaning It

Anne O'Gleadra

Chapter One

IN THIRD GRADE, I stuck not only my tongue but also both of my already-chapped lips to the bus-stop pole. I contribute this decision mainly to the fact that I was one of those starry-eyed, snow-crystal mesmerized, oblivious-to-everything (namely: other people, the future, and consequences) little kids. In third grade, my best friend was Dagen. Dagen, however, was not the friend who opted to help me out. Instead, he gathered up a little audience to holler and cackle at me as Lillian Paresky, with her big, sympathetic eyes and warm brown skin, finally ran to the teacher for help. And so, I fell in love with her, a love I eventually acted upon, kissing her at the school fun fair when we were sixteen.

Two years later, miserable and beyond sick of each other, Lillian and I were unhappily hitched. This was because I was always the kid whose parents made him do the right thing—or, at least, what they assumed that to be. I've never (before or since) seen Dagen as furious as he was on the day of my wedding: my best man, fuming and bitter. It was going to be my fault when our his-house garage band collapsed, because, despite my pleading promises, he knew just as well as I did that eight months later, as a clueless young father, I wouldn't know how to juggle things like high school and Lillian and a baby and a band.

A month and a day after that wedding, Lillian miscarried (aborted), annulled the wedding, claiming we hadn't consummated. Honestly, we hadn't. The little mock suite in my parents' basement just made Lils even more disgusted with me. The whole thing effectively ended my foray into romantic relationships and Dagen was the only person thrilled for me. He understood my happiness, my guilty relief.

So we called up Doug the Mute, our bassist, and Michael-called-Lucifer, our drummer, and resumed the jam sessions Dagen had called off out of loathing for me. We were like every other start-up sarcastic emo/pop-punk band there was, except for one thing: we actually made it. I was legitimately surprised. I had assumed we'd be hanging out, usually stoned, in Dagen's garage, until we finally got pissed at each other, or our parents forced us all off to college or into shitty full-time jobs.

Having known Dagen since preschool, however, had obviously desensitized me to his sickening charisma and bloodthirsty resoluteness. Apparently, Dag and Doug and Luce had known we would make it all along, but not me. I was totally blindsided. I am still jolted by the whole thing. Our band is called "You Wouldn't Get the Allusion Even if I Told it to you" and we write songs with similarly long names and (what we consider) witticisms. Our fan base, composed mostly of teenagers younger than our nineteen-year-old selves, who have dyed black hair, like ourselves, and many layers of try-hard clothing, call us *The Allusion* and leave it at that. YWGTAEIWTITY just isn't that great of an acronym.

Dagen was named by his mother, Miranda, in a fit of romanticism ten days after his birth. Miranda is a useless sort of lady filled with permissive, misguided love for her obnoxious only child. Until Dagen was eighteen, she lived mostly off the child support that faithfully came in from Dagen's otherwise disinterested patent lawyer father. And so, our mighty lead singer/guitarist strives to fulfill the glorious destiny that he claims accompanies anyone named Dagen Mercutio (Brown, but he never discloses his last name). This apparently translates into fucking anyone pretty and willing. He is our token heartbreaker: vibrant and smooth, unbearably extroverted and entirely crazy-making. Nevertheless, we all know we're here thanks to him, and we get free booze and weed and even girls who are exceptionally willing to sleep with our fairly loser-ish selves, so we don't really mind.

Let's be clear. Dagen is a complete asshole. He is also, for better or worse, my best friend. Given the competition, though, I'm not exactly surprised. Doug the Mute is a complete mystery to every one of us. He showed up at Dag's garage after we posted a "Bass Player wanted" poster—complete with a picture of an old man strumming a fish—at coffee shops and gig sites. He didn't call, he just showed up one day, instrument in hand. To this day, I do not know how he learned Dagen's address, but he kicks ass at what he does which makes up for the fact that he doesn't talk. We're fairly certain he can, although we've never legitimately tested him.

If we're asked in an interview or whatever to say five things about Doug, we can come up only with the following list: Doug the Mute snores every second night when we are on the road, he enjoys cheeseburgers, he's close to his family, will do anything once, and, apparently, is hung like a fucking walrus. At restaurants, he points vaguely to what he wants on the menu. He writes home once a week, usually sending gifts. He smiles occasionally. He's dependable. There's a website devoted to him, complete with a running thread written by all the chicks who've fucked him and loved it. It's more than a bit creepy, but I think (maybe?) he's silently smug about it.

Lucifer composes what we assume is Doug's missing half. He chatters constantly, is completely ADHD, and can drum for very long periods of time while maintaining a very, very fast rhythm—when he's on his meds. When he's off his meds, he can drum even faster, but for a way shorter amount of time. He and Dagen bicker constantly and viciously. Dagen always wins, and Luce always whines.

If Dagen is the heartthrob and Doug the muscly, silent type, and Luce the wiry hyperactive, I like to think of myself as the straight man, like, even-keeled or something. Dag prefers to dub me the pretty one and loves to expound on my "slender, almost feminine, beauty." I prefer to tell him to go fuck himself.

He and I write the songs together. We give Doug some melody and some lyrics, and he delivers a bass line, no problem—partially because he has a shit-ton of talent, and partially because our songs are seriously formulaic, mostly that catchy shit that is lapped up by radio and TV these days. We never claimed to want to be anything but sellouts, but every once in a while, Dag will pull some tender achy ballad out of his ass, singing it with such complete heartbreaking soul that he'll have half the auditorium running their eyeliner. I don't know where he gets that conviction from. People back home always ask me who the hell he's talking about—the fucking one he'll never get, the one who seems to occupy all those songs—and I never have a satisfying answer. Mostly I'm just getting really good at awkward shrugs. Our publicist, Rebecca, has forbidden me on pain of death from breaking it to them that Dagen's just good at reading people; he'll write what will sell.

Our first album was released at the beginning of last year, and sold better than even our label had hoped. Our second album, to everyone's surprise, except probably Dagen's, sold double our first. So now we're touring with it, selling out all over North America, leading hordes of little Allusion converts to coliseums across the continent. This is our *Better Than You* tour. Dagen penned that title. He never gets over himself. He doesn't need to.

***

What I'll never understand is how we came from a generation of grunge rock and punk, which was the stuff we used to cover when we first started up, and have since been transformed into a costumed, fake-eyelash-wearing, micro-manufactured masquerade of a show. Take right now, for instance: I'm in the wings wearing a bizarro sleeveless cut-up sweatshirt with cutoffs and a sweat band. I have sticky-gross lip gloss smeared across my lips and big pink circles painted on my cheeks. If I blink, I've got giant-ass eyes painted on my eyelids. The designer's vision is all about "living dollhouse circa 1980" or something. What exactly that has to do with our music, I couldn't tell you, but I've been told it's all about making it a real production.

Luce is how he always is: semi-long hair gelled into a Ken doll rock formation. He's shirtless and barefoot and wears electric blue and green 'eighties-style clamdiggers, evoking, I guess, a beach party at Barbie's. The crew is rapidly changing out the set from our latest opening band of the standard adjective-noun-name variety. They are pretty chill guys, but I haven't exactly invested myself in getting to know them. The audience is warmed up, ready for us. A dresser tugs at a thread hanging off of Luce's shorts and buzzes around us efficiently.

"Don't you look gorgeous, Benji." Dagen comes up behind me, whispering in my ear. I give him an elbow in the ribs.

"Fuck off. Don't call me that." It's a natural reaction now; there's only venom in my voice because of nerves which I never quite get over. This is our regimented pre-show banter. Lucifer is flitting around like a mosquito on acid, bouncing on his toes, humming randomly to himself. Doug does nothing. Dagen is standing too close to me, feeling superior, I'm sure. Nobody but him calls me that. Even my own mother calls me Ben or Benjamin. Dagen somehow gets away with it because we used to watch that toothless show on, like, PBS or whatever when we were younger. About the mutt dog that always came to the rescue? *Benji.*

So. yeah. Only Dagen, and never when other people might hear. I think he worries someone else might hear and start using it (I worry about that same thing), and that would throw a kink in his great scheme of originality. Dagen wanders away again, planting his teeth into Luce's shoulder cordially. Luce is so caught up in jittering, he doesn't even notice. The same non-reaction from Doug. How can they be so isolated? Once upon a time, I think maybe I could ignore Dagen's demands for attention, but now he makes a point of refusing to be ignored.

***

Sometime after the mouth-on-bus-stop-pole thing, Dagen decided he wanted a protégé: namely, me. He started dragging me around to his house every day. Yelling at his mom to bring up snacks, he would yank me by the arm up the stairs to his room where he would promptly show me all the stuff he had and then sneer at all the stuff I had. Luckily, I was a fairly disconnected little kid. While he would tear into me for having a *Ninja Turtles* backpack when the *3 Ninjas* were "way more rad," I'd tune him out in favour of making up silent stories about his *Transformers*. I'd be quite content in this right up until he'd bite me. He's always been a biter.

I wasn't really a violent kid, so far as eight-year-old kids go, but his teeth would always find that spot on my shoulder, and I would feel obliged to try to kick his ass. We'd wrestle on the floor for a while, usually until I started to cry. Then we'd eat the snack that call-me-Miranda-Honey would leave outside the door while I pouted over whatever wound had finally sent me over the edge. Dag would distract me by fucking with his food, sticking cheese strings up his nose, or squirting yogurt tubes at my face, or with rousing games of "See? Food!" until I cheered up. Then we'd start the whole insult-bite-cry cycle again. By the second round, I would usually march from his room in search of the phone, intent on calling my parents and tearfully begging them to come pick me up. But Dagen always had other ideas. Somehow, by the time my mom or dad picked up the phone, Dagen would have managed to convince me to ask to stay for dinner, instead.

Usually, the answer was no. My parents are both level-headed psychologists who have child-rearing down to an art, or, at least, to a textbook. A literal textbook, to be honest. My brother Trenton and I were raised to behave, do well in school, have self-esteem, but also respect authority and work hard in all we undertook. My folks knew that Dagen was a bad influence on me; however, they were also left-leaning Social Democrats intent on making sure I was exposed to human diversity, and apparently, Dagen's wild-child, single-unemployed-mother household fit their criteria. And so, despite what I'm certain was their better judgment, they encouraged the association, making sure I occasionally brought Dag around for well-cooked, organic meals and appropriate dinnertime conversation. He really got a kick out of them. And, in time, they learned to reciprocate the sentiment; my mother even lets Dag refer to her as Ms. W., and not, as she typically prefers, the gender-nonspecific Dr. Walard (not to be confused with my dad, who is Dr. Walkens. Trenton and I are Walard-Walkenses and it is the worst).

On the occasions that I was permitted to spend the evening at Dagen's, I would be mesmerized by the parade of processed foods—pizza pops, swallowed down with Coke and followed up by bubble-gum ice cream, and Dunkaroos—things strictly forbidden at my house. Afterwards, he and I would watch child-unfriendly TV while Miranda read her romance novels in the living room.

"Watch this!" Dagen would say, as the *NYPD Blue* guys drew their guns. "Those shit-heads are going to get it!" My eyes would expand in horror. At my house, we only watched *Benji*.

***

I guess it's my turn. Dagen nips at the scarred spot on my shoulder, grinning, knowing the scar is his own doing. We were ten. He came out with a black eye; I came out with a tetanus shot. He still thinks it's funny. My parents really didn't.

"Play a good show, Benji," he says in that secret voice I know he reserves for me.

"Yeah, yeah. You, too."

"Oh, I will." He grins cockily at me.

We walk out. And everyone starts screaming.

Oh, yeah.

This is why we do this.

Chapter Two

"T HIS IS A song," Dagen explains between songs, "for that one girl..." I look at him and realize he's stalking towards me. I hold my guitar up a bit higher, like some sort of a buffer. Doug produces a threatening, reverberating sound on his bass as Dagen reaches me and, heedless of my guitar, slides a hand onto my hip. The crowd fucking screams. I blush beneath my stage makeup even though this is all rehearsed. Apparently, homoeroticism gives fans a real charge, and we have been encouraged to cater to it a little. But somehow Dagen missed the memo on the "a little" bit. Or ignored it completely.

Either way, he feels the need to kick it up a notch with every show. It used to just be a teasing, seductive glance, and then came the walk, and now, apparently, a touch. It's kind of uncomfortable, and I know I show it, because there's a bit of a gap between my low-riding shorts and my shirt, and his hand is right there, and he's looking right into my eyes, making me blush brighter than the damn circles on my cheeks because he's being so fucking ridiculous and his palm is skimming my skin like I'm something to be desired. And the screams are growing louder.

"That won't leave your thoughts alone..." he continues, "and all you want to do..." He brings his mouth towards my neck. Motherfucking Dagen. I know he thinks it's funny when I get awkward like this, so unlike him. Even with Lillian, I wasn't a hand-holding, brush-up-against-you kind of guy. (Which is why I think Lillian liked me in the first place—I was her little I'll-make-you-socially-healthy project.) Dagen's fake eyelashes flutter against the skin beneath my ear. God. Isn't he done yet? He's really fucking milking this.

"Bite her fucking head off?" He grins, turning his face to the crowd. Everyone laughs, the girls scream some more, hoping for lip action. I swear, there is *nothing* wrong with a guy liking some girl-on-girl porn if they can get rowdy over this little bit of play.

I start up with the notes, lucky that they hadn't gone totally out of my head with Dagen being so goddamn hammy, and then he starts in.

"You're sick and you're twisted..."

***

I'm not totally clueless. I accept the fact that the relationship between Dagen and I is one of codependence. I'm easygoing about practically everything, with the exception of this little stunt he's currently pulling. He's short-tempered and moody and arrogant and determined to get what he wants when he wants it. He's got that indisputably popular thing about him, one that draws people to him, makes them want to be like him, or be with him, and he knows it absolutely. But I'm the only one who can stand him for any period of time, not that anyone ever gets the chance to stand him because he inevitably drops them for the next hippest thing.

And he knows that, too. I put up with all his shit, and he, therefore, doesn't lay too much of his shit directly on me. I have some sort of immunity to his insulting nature. He knows that, for all his charisma, he would be useless without my sometimes much-needed diplomacy. He needs me to step in when he's grouchy and pissing people off, and I'm happy to do it because he's the reason we made it in the first place.

It's kind of creepy how charming he can be. When he meets somebody in the industry, he somehow has just enough friendly-but-aloof appeal to make that person straight up want to be his best friend. And then he spends days and nights with that person, coming back with outrageous stories of his varying adventures—

the parties, the drugs, the orgies, the four a.m. escapades. It's fucking ridiculous. For a few weeks, this person will be his world, until he meets the next person, but the first person inevitably takes a long time to get the message. They're still crushing on him, calling him, wanting him, and he's gone. He's got what he wanted, and now, they're used-up, boring. And somehow, they are left knowing just that.

He used to bring me along and introduce me to every beautiful, ambitious person he'd ever met—sometimes it seemed like he'd met them all—but I didn't dig it. I'd rather be at home, or in the bus or hotel if we're on the road, reading or playing video games or chilling with Doug and Luce at a pub, maybe talking with a nice-looking girl who wants to fuck me. Because all those beautiful people don't give a fuck about me, and I don't give a fuck about them, but we all give a fuck about Dagen.

Sometimes I'm actually terrified that I'm just another victim of Dagen's charm; that he is doing exactly the same thing to me as he does to all his conquests—minus the fucking and the crazy nights—just priming me for his usage. Then again, unlike pretty much everyone else in his life, he never stopped calling me. He never stopped needing me to calm him down. And he's careful with me, it makes me feel stable enough that I keep providing for him like that. Fuck it. He makes me feel special, and his attention is a goddamn drug.

I'm just guessing, here, psychoanalyzing like only the child of two shrinks can, but I have to be careful, because, like everyone else on this fucking planet, I think I might be a little bit in love with Dagen Mercutio, and that is the opposite of a safe place to be.

***

"*You rely on God or love to save you/but I know that Neverland doesn't exist.*" Dagen keens because sometimes, though rarely, his lyrics are more than just lyrics. They are things that he actually

11

thinks. Dagen is a raging cynic. He thinks people who fall in love are just fooling themselves, that they are just victims of the corporate machinations which peddle merchandise under the label of love.

It pissed him off so bad when I told him I loved Lillian. He was so angry, he wouldn't speak to me for a week. It was pretty intense. 'Course, he gloated over it when things started to fall apart. He gets off on making people feel stupid, little, inferior, and he's good at it. But at the same time, he can make you feel so singled out, so...appreciated. It's his shtick. He can have anyone, and he does. So, of course, I refuse to let him have me.

My biggest fear, therefore, is Dagen finding out. Not that I might be kind of gay...because honestly, he wouldn't care. He'd just call me a total fag in that serious-except-not-at-all-serious way of his and laugh because it's not like he's at all particular about the gender of the people he fucks. No, I'm afraid he might find out that I might be into *him*. And so I'm very, very careful. He can't know. He'd—Fuck. I don't even know what he would do. But I would end up with a soul torn to pulp, and that's honestly the only scenario I can see playing out. So I fuck a lot of women and try to ignore the nauseous-needy feeling in my gut that seizes up when he put his hands (or teeth) on me.

***

After the show, Doug and Luce and I are flopped out on a couch backstage, stinking and exhausted (even Lucifer yawns) and Dagen sprawls across our laps dramatically.

"Nice show, gentlemen," he condescends, as if we put on the whole thing to please him. We shove him off onto the floor. "What the fuck!" He scrambles, but then grins, adrenaline his favourite drug of all. "Shall we go meet the adoring masses?"

***

Lots of people I've met in this industry complain about being celebrities. It's awesome for about a day, and then they realize they'd maybe rather be left the fuck alone, and I get that. Dagen, however, was meant for show business. He is a total publicity whore. He loves having people love him. People screaming his name and begging him to sign their breasts makes his life just that much better. Our publicist adores him for it.

Doug the Mute stands around sullenly, sizing up the girls before him asking for autographs/offering him their bodies. He gives one a lazy grin, nods at her, takes a swig of his beer and leaves, her tottering after him on too-high heels.

Dagen is talking animatedly to a large group of emo kids, all very obviously thrilled to be meeting him in the flesh and finding out that he really is That Cool in person, just like all the Dagen-inspired blogs promise.

"So, you guys like the show?" he asks, casually, casting where he knows he'll hook.

"Oh my god, yes!" comes the general response. A gaggle of teenagers follow us onto the bus. I pull out some beers from our mini fridge and pass them around, ignoring Doug and his girl making out (and then some) on a cushion near the back.

I make casual small talk with some of the kids who followed us on. They're nice enough, overexcited, overly awed. I'm not totally convinced that any of the girls are old enough for me to risk fucking them, at least not since we're in Columbus. Dagen is tyrannical about only fucking people who are of-age. It's hardly an ethical concern, he is more just tyrannical about everything that might mar our image. "If you can find one who's sixteen, you can find one of the same who is eighteen," is his party line. And none of us ever feel up to weathering the wrath of Dagen, so mostly we obey.

"Are you guys fucking ready to have some fun?" Dagen announces loudly; he's still performing. Everyone laughs and commits to getting hammered.

A few beers and blunts in and I'm hazy. Our bus pulls into our hotel parking lot, and we make our way, too loud, and too rude, up to our suite. Doug is having sloppy sex on a couch nearby, but we're all drunk enough to not really care. Lucifer is high as a fucking kite, skittering around, laughing hysterically with some fans. Dagen is talking in a low, serious-style voice with a girl and a guy in the corner, showing them his philosophical side—which, ironically, is just as superficial as his shallow side. Soon, they'll all be screwing on a hotel bed in the room next to mine.

Six a.m. rolls around; I'm starting to come down, now just tired. I politely kick everyone out and go to bed. It's all just a big repeat of the last year, and it dawns on me that maybe I'm a relationship kind of guy. I'm getting bored of hookups already. I'm too reserved to have sober random sex, and drunken random sex just isn't that good. Maybe after this tour, I'll get myself a girlfriend. It's not like I want to be married—possibly ever again—but I want something steady. A laid-back girl who's cool with me being on the road, sends me nice messages in the morning, and is sympathetic to me whining about Dagen. It'll just be easier.

I try to sleep to the not-so-sweet sounds of Dagen and his fans fucking noisily: whiny, repetitive moans and throaty grunts. Dagen making no attempt to muffle the sounds of his pleasure. "Yes, baby, *Yes. Right fucking there!*"

Well. If this band thing doesn't pan out, he'll always have a future in porn.

I reach into the drawer next to my bed and chuck the bible at the offending wall. "Dagen. It's six in the fucking morning," I call out.

I hear the grunting peak. Twice. Then, finally, Dagen shouts back at me, happily, "Sorry, Ben!"

"No, you're not," I reply, and I hear the three of them laugh, some moving around, and more muffled voices, until they're in the hallway outside my closed door.

"No, seriously, you guys. I want to stay in touch. This night has been unreal." I hear Dagen through the wall, and he sounds serious enough that I feel a pathetic pang of jealousy that really should know better by now.

"Oh my god. This has seriously been, like, the most incredible night of my whole freakin' life. Like. You felt it, right?" comes a reply. The girl, I think.

"Fuck, yeah, I felt it. Jesus, Cori, you are something else, you know that?"

I roll my eyes. That's Dagen for you.

"I so wish you could stay, but we've gotta hit the road early, and we're all assholes when we wake up, so I'm going to give you some cab money, alright, Cori?" He says her name too often with too much sincerity. "Jon'll make sure you get home okay, right, babe?"

Jon murmurs something I don't catch. It makes my stomach roil with second-hand guilt, or maybe just more jealousy, I can't tell.

Some more kissing sounds and the hotel door opening and closing. Silence.

Of course, a few minutes later, Dag is in my room, boxers riding low on his hips, smelling of sweat and sex. He collapses next to me on the bed with a satisfied sigh.

"Have fun?" I mumble.

"You bet," he answers.

"Does it burn when you pee?"

"Benji, are you slut-shaming me?" he accuses, mock-scandalized and lapping a lazy backhand against my ass.

I grunt affirmatively.

He rolls over, flinging his arms above his head and sighing contentedly. "She let me fuck her ass while he fucked mine. It was a goddamn Christmas miracle."

"Well, Merry February Christmas, then."

"Mmm," he agrees, fading fast. "'Night, Benji…"

"Night, fuckwit."

**

15

It's breakfast. Early morning, and we're at some shitty truck stop—waffles and strong coffee and acetaminophen. Dagen's bored. I can tell because he won't stop kicking me under the table. He's antsy, wants to get on the road. How nice of him to let me know.

"Fuck off, Dagen," I tell him, more tired than anything.

"What?" He jumps at the chance of an altercation.

"Stop kicking me."

"I thought it was the table leg!" he lies.

"No, you really didn't."

"Oh, because you get to tell me what I think now?" he bites back at me.

"Yup. I'm omnipotent like that," I reply, keeping my tone casual, not synching up with his animosity.

"Oh, sorry, what I meant to say was, you don't fucking get to tell me what I think is what."

"Let's just get the fuck out of here." I sigh. I'm so not having this right now.

"Guys," Luce starts in, the fake-maple syrup finally jolting him back into wakefulness. "Guys, man, dude, that show last night was fucking awesome. Holy shit, did you see those double-pierced tits? The girl on the guy's shoulders? Man, I thought I'd fucking lose my shit. Fuck, I wish she'd been around after the show. I wanted to see if she had a matching set on her snatch…"

"You did bring her back with you, Lucifer, you fucking shitwad," I cut in. "You guys were screwing on the bathroom floor while everyone was trying to take a piss."

"You serious? Fuck." Lucifer mourns, "How come you get to remember it and not me?"

"Would you shut up, Helner?" Dagen's voice is sharp.

"Yeah. Yeah. Right. Sorry, Dag. Sorry, man."

"Don't be sorry. Shut your mouth."

I feel like I should cut in here, tell Lucifer that he doesn't need to take any shit from Dagen. But honestly, I'm just glad when he shuts the fuck up.

***

On the bus, we sleep. We'll be here for a good seven or eight hours before we reach wherever the hell it is we're going. I can't keep track anymore. As long as Dagen knows so he can shout out the typical shit about how this is for sure the best crowd he has ever encountered, and how he absolutely does not say this to every crowd, and how great Detroit or Lansing or Des Moines is, then we're all good. But now I'm curious.

"Where the fuck are we headed, anyways?" I ask.

"Uh…" Luce offers helpfully.

"Shut it, Luce." Dagen doesn't even let him start. "Toronto."

"Toronto…?" Luce opens it anyway.

"God, you're a fucking moron. It's in Canada, dickless."

"Hey! Fuck you, Dag!"

"I said shut up. You're so goddamn annoying."

"Maybe you could both shut up," I interject. "Silent Bob over there looks like he's going to splice your spleens with a spork."

"Nice alliteration there, Benjamin," Dagen says, quasi-sarcastically.

"Thanks. I try. Good night."

"It's morning," Lucifer informs us.

"Shut UP, Helner," Dagen repeats more forcefully.

"Fine. Jesus. You don't have to be so bitchy about it—"

A Coke can flies over, nicking Lucifer in the head. He gets the message. We all zone back out. Life on the road.

***

Days get boring sort of fast. Around one, when we've all slept about as much as we're going to, I fish out some music. We buy a lot of music these days. As musicians, I feel like it's somehow our civic duty to listen to as much new shit as we can, or something. Have opinions. We'll listen to an album ten times and then figure out if we like it or not. It pisses Dagen off that I'm so meticulous about stuff like this...but there's not a heck of a lot else to do. Besides, he likes to be abreast of what is selling well, so his whining is mostly just for my benefit more than anything.

I put in *I'm Wide Awake, It's Morning.* Oberst does it for me. Less so for Dagen. There's a good possibility I put it in because I know he's in a pissy mood, and sometimes, I like to rile him up a bit. He glares at me but sits back with his eyes closed. In the end, he's pretty serious about this shit, too.

Lucifer has talked Doug into a game of Go Fish, which is really something to watch. The Mute has a specific signal for each card, which Luce has worked hard at decoding. For example, if Doug taps the tabletop with his left ring finger, it means "Do you have a red eight?" He licks his lips when he's looking for a black queen. A condescending look means "Go fucking fish."

Somehow there are stakes involved, and I watch them for a while.

Dagen cracks an eye open to look at me. "You look terrible. You've still got makeup everywhere. Didn't you shower?"

I shrug. I'm no good at mornings. "I'll shower when we get there."

"No wonder this fucking bus stinks all the time."

"Jesus. Someone's bitchy," I needle, knowing it really won't help things. "And the bus stinks because nobody ever bothers to throw out their garbage. It has nothing to do with me, asswipe."

"Fuck you, you don't clean up your shit, either."

"I will at the next stop. Now shut up. Listen to the music."

"I hate his voice."

"So focus on the instruments."

Dagen finally smiles. "You and your little obsessions, Benji... it's cute, really."

"You're an asshole," I say without anything resembling conviction.

"Yes, yes I am," Dag replies proudly. We return our focus to the album.

"What's this track called?" Dagen asks after a while, his voice—finally, thankfully—geared back to friendly.

I scramble for the jewel case. "'Lua.'"

"Hm. Reminds me of you."

I raise an eyebrow. "'The love I sell you'? What, am I your hooker now, Dag?"

"Ha-fucking-ha. I meant more the *skinny like a model eyes all painted black* bit."

"Your eyes are painted just as often as mine," I retort.

"Yeah, but I have a little thing called muscle mass. That, and I wash my face."

I'm too hungover to form a response. And "fuck off" feels overused by this point.

Dagen mistakes my silence for offense.

"I'm jk, Benji, God."

"I'm not mad!" I protest.

"Then what's with the silent treatment?"

"I'm just listening to the song!"

"Sure you are."

I glare at him, look around for something to throw, but he's ahead of me, and pegs me with his shoe.

"Your shoe, Dagen? What the actual fuck?" I throw it back, but he's smiling already. Oh good, I've put him in a better mood without even trying.

I sigh. I hate travelling. I feel all…groggy all the time. I return my attention to Doug and Luce. Luce, apparently, is winning. That doesn't happen very often. Doug the Mute doesn't look too happy. Then again, he rarely looks happy. I glare at Dagen, and he gives me one of those grins he relies on to stop people from being pissed off at him. I hate that it works on me.

"Connect Four?" he asks innocently.

"If I can go first."

"What're the stakes?"

"Bright Eyes. All week."

"Versus MCR all week?"

"Fuck, no."

"Blink?"

"They broke up, man. Don't you get that?"

"They're my security blanket." He almost pouts, I swear.

"Fine. But I'm vetoing Pants and Jacket."

"Fair."

***

I win. Dag just doesn't have the patience for board games. He gets distracted and zones out. He'll be bitching by tomorrow about the music, and I'll probably let him change it, but for today, I can enjoy my melancholy tunes in peace. I sit back in my seat to do so.

"What are you doing?" Dagen pesters.

"Enjoying my victory."

"I'm bored."

"I'm shocked." I'm not, in fact, even slightly shocked.

"Tell me something interesting."

"Oh, yes, Dagen, let me appease you by any means necessary and keep you entertained like a goddamn two-year-old. Actually, on second thoughts, seriously fuck off."

"Bennnnn," he whines.

"Oh, fine. Pick a movie."

I turn off the music, drag out my laptop and put in the DVD Dagen tosses at me without bothering to look at what it is. He comes to sit next to me on the wide couch-ish thing attached to the floor. I put the laptop on one end, leaning it inwards so it won't fall down.

"I can't see," Dagen feels the need to inform me.

"So, move so you can see."

Dagen grumbles. He doesn't like that I don't acquiesce to his every want. But I know he'd like it even less if I did. He gets back at me by shoving himself too close into me. I hate that I love the warmth of him squashing into my side. I'm afraid that he knows it, and I try to ignore it. Almost before the opening credits are finished, he's asleep with his goddamn head on my goddamn shoulder. Using my foot, I close the laptop, and copy his example. Not a heck of a lot else to do, anyway.

Just outside Toronto, we stop for dinner.

"Good morning, Benji, you little queer," Dagen murmurs pleasantly to me when I wake up to the cessation of motion. My head's resting over his and my sleeping self thought it was a good idea to curl a hand around his leg, just above his knee. Luckily, it's Dagen, and this is hardly the most embarrassing thing I've ever done around him. I shove him good-naturedly on his ass.

"That's gonna bruise," he sniffs.

"Good thing you like it rough," I reply, unsympathetic.

Laughing, Dagen straightens himself out and stands up. "Think anyone will recognize me in there?" he asks, hopefully.

"God, I hope not. If I have to listen to your nauseating fan-banter, I'm not going to be able to eat."

"What kind of banter would you prefer?"

"The silent kind."

"Aren't you clever today?"

"Kicked your ass at Connect Four."

"Your parents will be so proud—what was it they said about us? 'If you're going to pursue this career, apply your whole self, boys.' I can see you really took those words to heart—right down to en route board games."

"Obviously. Hence the me-winning part."

Dagen laughs again and shoves his shoulder playfully into mine—enough to make me stumble stupidly in the parking lot.

***

The restaurant is a hole. I scarf my burger quickly, Lucifer having found a highly impressive string of babble to fill our half hour with. Honestly, we've been everywhere with him. He cannot possibly have any new anecdotes to tell us, and yet, somehow, he always has something to say. I think, though I couldn't say for sure, that I catch a hint of amusement in Doug the Mute's eye. At least someone finds the situation not completely horrible. I, personally, want to take a bazooka to Luce's brains.

We get back on the bloody stupid bus. I force everyone to take out their garbage. We need a fucking Laundromat. We stink. We're groggy as shit. We look about as bad as we feel. In four hours, we'll be onstage, and the idea is enough to make me wish I was anywhere else.

Chapter Three

OUR TOUR WILL be finished in two more weeks, and despite the hours of tedium, it still kind of feels like a blur. Thankfully, there haven't been any new startling advances, unless you count Dagen actually connecting his chapsticked lips to my neck onstage in Chicago, which elicited a fucking full-throttle orgasmic cacophony from the crowd. I hate that I let him fuck with me like this. I want to talk to him about it, but I can pretty much predict his response. "It's just a part of the show!" and "What...do I make you...uncomfortable, Benji?" I can picture him, homing in on me, hot breath on my neck in a repeat of his past performances. It'll be good for me to have the break from him. Not that he'll give me one. Honestly, after, like, two days at home in Seattle, I guarantee he'll call me up, claiming boredom and forcing me to leave my blanket and tea cocoon.

***

It's night and I'm in a post-show stupor. We skipped out on the fan-greeting after tonight's show, opting instead for collapsing into our bunks on the bus. We have a new destination tomorrow and we need to drive all night. I thought I was asleep but am suddenly highly aware of movement from across the bus—more specifically, from Dagen's bunk.

"Dagen, if you're fucking jerking off, I'm going to strangle you with your own intestines."

"Mmm, Benji," he says evilly. "Would it help if I told you I'm thinking about you?"

"Can you seriously not survive one fucking night without some sort of sexual fulfillment?"

"I could, but I don't really want to…"

"Can you at least take it to the bathroom?"

"Yeah, because nothing gets me going like a freezing bus bathroom that literally reeks of formaldehyde. You're such a prude, Ben. It's not like you don't do the exact same thing…"

"I at least try and wait until everyone is asleep!" I protest.

"Oh, Benji," he chides, "I wouldn't dream of sleeping through the delectable orchestra that is your palm on your dick."

I blush. "Jesus, Dagen. Fuck off, would you?"

"Hypocrite. I was trying, but nooo, it would offend the delicate sensibilities of pure little Benjamin."

"You know what I meant."

"Fine." He pulls his hands up, showing them both to me. "Happy?"

I turn towards the wall. "Sure."

The next thing I know, Dagen's worming his way under my covers. He slips his hand mock-romantically up my side, causing me to jump.

"What the fuck, Dag?" I hiss.

"What?" he asks, innocent as pie.

"What are you doing?"

He brushes a piece of my hair behind my ear.

"Nothing," he answers, finally.

"Get the fuck off me. I'm sleeping."

"I knew you were awake," he whispers. The words aren't hot, but his breath is.

"I was not. I was perfectly contented in my sleeping state."

"Were not. Your breathing was too shallow."

"You were listening to my breathing? Because that's not creepy at all."

"It's Doug's snoring's night off." Dagen shrugs. "And I'm bored."

"You're always fucking bored. Can't you entertain yourself somehow?"

"I tried, but you vetoed that." He grinds into me, and I can feel his dick, still semi-hard, pressing into my ass.

"Dagen! God! What the fuck are you doing? You know this is like legitimate assault, right?"

"Mmm." Dagen doesn't sound that concerned. "I'm just showing you that you pretty much ruined my night."

"Fine. Go jerk off." I sigh. "I don't fucking care. Just get the hell out of my bed."

He nuzzles my neck. He's always pulling shit like this, and I know I shouldn't let him, or at least make more than a token effort to stop him. But I don't even try; not really. I wonder sometimes if I, like, used a serious voice or approached him about it and was all *dude, I seriously need you to back off...* Actually, I don't wonder. I know he would. Even Dagen can respect firmly asserted boundaries. So, of course, I never set any. I feel like a twelve-year-old girl at a pool party, squealing about not being thrown in the water when all she really wants is just that.

"Mmm, maybe I want to stay," Dagen murmurs into my trapezius.

I growl.

He laughs.

"Oh, fine, Benji, have it your way." His teeth find my neck, biting gently. "I love you..." His voice is teasing, prodding.

"Yeah, yeah, love you, too, you stupid fuck. Now get lost."

I practically hear him grin as he crosses the aisle to his bunk. I try to ignore him as he beats off, but he knows I'm listening. "Oh, Benji..." he whimpers.

"Dagen, SHUT UP!"

He laughs as he comes.

"Benjamin, you are lucky you had me in middle school. The cool kids wouldn't have left you alone, otherwise."

"I have no idea what you are even talking about," I reply tiredly.

"You're just so fucking easy to bother."

"You're just so fucking easy."

"No complaints yet," he answers smugly.

"I hope you get chlamydia and die."

"Mmm. Wish I could say the feeling is mutual, Benj..." He peters off, his breaths coming slow and even.

God, the guy can fall asleep so easily. Me...not so much.

***

Just three shows to go before we're finished, and the heating breaks down. Of course it does, because it's the middle of fucking winter, and we're travelling up to another town in fucking Canada. Dag is fucking psyched to go because he knows they don't get a lot of concerts, and the hicks will thus adore him. The rest of us are loathe to go, halfway convinced we'll see igloos before we even get there.

It's March. It is *late* March, and it is still fucking cold. We spend all day huddled under six layers of clothing and blankets doing a heck of a lot of nothing: too cold to put on movies or CDs or do anything but sit around and whine. We hate to leave the Tim Horton's we stop at for dinner, because it means leaving warmth, but we don't have much of a choice. It's getting dark already. Who fucking lives in a place like this? This is veritably uninhabitable. I curl into my bed on the bus again. And even fall asleep.

A few hours later, with the Mute snoring and Luce muttering madly to himself in his sleep, Dagen again finds it necessary to invade my personal space for the forty billionth time.

"What the fuck are you doing?" I murmur, blurry and exhausted, as he burrows selfishly into my nest of quilts and sweaters.

"If I kept a running tally of how many times you ask me that a day..." he quips, his teeth chattering.

"Fuck off."

"You say that a lot, too." He snuggles closer. I remain stoically unimpressed. "I'm cold, Ben."

"That's because you only have one blanket on your bunk, because you have never learned—nor likely ever will learn—how to pack responsibly, despite my helpful hints and suggestions."

"You have four blankets," he replies, ignoring my grumbling. "Give me one."

"I like my blankets. All of them."

"C'mon, I just need one."

I turn my back on him, hoping he'll screw off or maybe hoping he won't.

I suddenly feel hands like liquid nitrogen tuck up under my hoodie and connect with the skin on my back.

"Shit! Jesus Christ, Dagen!"

"I told you I was cold."

"What did you do? Hold your hands against the window or something?"

"Dunno," he mumbles. I roll over to face him. Unfortunately, he keeps his hands on my skin, and now they're on my stomach, still freezing.

"Move!"

"You're warm," he whines.

"Because I'm not stupid enough to only pack one blanket or cuddle up against the goddamn glass!"

He just gives me a pitiful look.

Exasperated, I grab his fingers in mine, forcing them outside of my hoodie. I start rubbing one of his hands between my own in some stereotypical attempt to generate circulation. He immediately presses his other hand back under my clothes, curled against my hip where it coaxes goose bumps all over my skin. Eventually, I get his hands warmed up.

"Will you go away now?" I ask.

"If I go away, I'll just be back later…" He sighs, and doesn't leave, just rolls over, so his back is towards me. Grumbling, I do the same, our backs solidly connected in the tiny bunk. Soon, he's warmer than blankets.

***

When I wake up next, the bastard is spooning me. I jerk over onto my back, violently, only to catch sight of his grinning blue eyes.

"What are you doing?" I sigh.

"I woke up, and…you were just begging to be spooned…" He nuzzles my neck, like he did a few weeks ago. I put on a show of trying to shove him off, but he's stronger than me, and at a better angle. He moves his efforts upwards, sliding his nose against my jaw and cheek and…lips. I can't move. I'm maybe possibly literally paralyzed. This is what I want and what I don't want more than anything else in the world.

"Could you not?" I finally force out, my voice low.

But he doesn't stop. His lips find my ear, which is a bad thing, a very bad thing, for me. Because my ears are very…sensitive. By which I mean, I'm hard within the minute. And my brain is telling me, *he can't find out. Dagen cannot know.* I get that. So, I somehow manage to roll over again, my back to him, vulnerable, but at least now he won't feel my hard-on. Jesus, what is wrong with me? His teeth are tugging at my earlobe, then his lips and… God, is that his tongue? Smoothing over it, he's working upwards, the tip of his fucking tongue delicately tracing the shell of my ear. His hand is on my hip, on the bare skin, again. He's always there.

"Quit it, Dagen," I say, helplessly, elbowing backwards.

After a bit more suckling, he finally does. "You're no fun at all," he murmurs, repositioning himself, draping one arm possessively over my chest.

"I'm just not a fucking fag." I know I'm being childish.

"Watch your mouth," he replies placidly.

I ignore him. I don't feel like I can do anything else.

I feel his lips along my mastoid and then on the back of my neck for just a second. I try and get some sleep.

Later, cold light streams in the windows. I'm alone, Dagen sleeping soundly in his own bunk. I convince myself that it was just a fucked-up dream.

At least, I do until Dagen gives me that frickin' sly grin when he wakes to find me staring at him.

***

When we reach the hotel, I shower. Afterwards, quickly combing out my hair in the mirror, I notice at tiny hickey behind my ear.

Fuck.

Chapter Four

I MANAGE TO SURVIVE the tour. Back home, in Seattle, I curl up and die in my room. Or I try. I hibernate for three days straight in my small, neat apartment where everything is set up exactly how I want it. The entirety of my possessions outside of furniture can fit easily into one room. I hate clutter; it stresses me out. Dagen says I'm anal. I say I just don't like a bunch of shit all over the place.

My place is pretty modernish, I guess. I didn't design it, but I liked the open spaces and square faucets. I've basically converted one whole wall of my living room into a huge floor-to-ceiling CD rack. The albums are arranged alphabetically by artist— something Dagen refuses to get over, because it means every time I buy a new one, I have to shift them all down. It's a process I find kind of soothing, but try explaining that to Dag. Outside of the CDs, and a good stereo, I don't have much: a TV, an old-school Nintendo with four games plus Duck Hunt, my iPod, appliances, and basic necessities, and six or seven guitars. I walk a lot. Sleep more. Eat food that doesn't come from a diner.

***

It's been a week, and I am still sleeping until two everyday. Make myself pancakes or bacon and eggs every "morning." Don't phone anyone.

So, of course, my phone rings.

"Hey, Mom," I answer.

"How long have you been home?" she asks. To the point, that's my mom.

"Just a couple of days…" I lie. A little.

"Well, your father and I would have liked to have heard from you."

"Yeah, sorry. I was…tired."

"Are you sick?"

"What? No."

"Well, can we expect you for dinner tonight, then?"

"Uh…"

"Seven, then. Bring Dagen. I'm sure neither of you have had anything decent to eat for months."

"Okay, Mom. Seven. We'll be there. Love you."

"Love you, too."

I've probably had that exact conversation, like, eighty thousand times in my life.

***

Dagen, apparently, had anticipated my phone call. He picks up after one ring.

"When's dinner?"

"Seven."

"Excellent. Any chance it'll include asparagus?" Dagen loves asparagus. I think it's the closest thing he's had to a real relationship.

"My folks love you more than Trenton and I combined. Of course there'll be asparagus."

"Don't beat yourself up about it. I'm just more irresistible than you. It can't be helped."

"How's Miranda?" I ask.

"She quit Buddhism, she's trying out God again."

"I thought he failed her? Didn't help her to quit smoking?"

"Well, God loves her even if she smokes, turns out."

"I don't get it."

"You never do, Benji." He sighs, but cheerfully, and there's a hint of something I don't understand. "So," he continues, "do you want me to come pick your poor, car-less self up, then?"

"That would defeat the purpose of me not having a car." It's an environmental thing. He knows it.

"I'll be there at six."

He hangs up. I go for a walk.

***

After a pointedly uneventful dinner at my parents' house, from which Dagen and I both received masses of Tupperwared leftovers, I go online, aimlessly trekking though the "Prospective Students" pages of various college websites. I feel it coming on: that antsy, uncomfortable question of What Am I Here For. Trenton is working on a PhD in applied linguistics and I…I'm not stupid enough to think that emo bands don't have an expiry date. Music genres don't work like that, and frankly, I am not exactly amazingly talented. I know my instrument and all, but I'm riding this thing on the coattails of Dagen's charisma. I think even he can admit that we're not gonna be the next Radiohead or U2 or whatever. We're not gonna last forever. And when all this ends, all I will have to show for it is an overdependence on weed, an obscure Wikipedia page, and a mostly sore heart.

I poke around the entry requirements. Nothing too stringent. Hell, it looks like come September, I could be enrolled in a course or two. The label's pushing for another album, so we'll be recording sometime this summer, then likely on the road again come January, so it is feasible. I cruise through the course calendar. Nothing jumps out at me, but something's gotta be better than nothing, right? I determine to at least get my shit together enough to apply.

***

Dagen, apparently, shares my unease. He schedules a band practice for the next day. The edgy tone of his voice made all of us agree to show, though I doubt any of us really wanted to.

"I have a new song," Dagen informs us.

He grabs a ball of loose leaf from his pockets and sets about uncrumpling it. It's thick, with a pained sort of wistfulness, and he's got a melody which is easy enough to transcribe to guitar. We set to fiddling around with it for a while, Doug offering up a baseline in no time and even Luce seems on task. The whole thing is gelling nicely. It needs some tweaking, but it is definitely a song. We take a break, feeling good, when Lucifer takes it upon himself to inform us that he doesn't really love it.

"Oh, really, Lucifer?" Dagen is circling in on him, dangerous as a starving hyena. Doug and I eye each other nervously. "You have a problem with my songwriting ability?"

Luce should be shitting himself. Dag's got that whole epic eye-glint thing going on. He's pretty fucking serious about his music, and he's got the artist's ego, like, you gotta be careful. Too bad Lucifer has negative intuition.

"What?" Luce replies. "Fuck, no. I like what you write just fine. I just wish I had something faster..." His hands fiddle with his sticks like a whirligig. Without knowing it, he's eluded death. Virtually any other answer and Dagen would've flown at him, regardless of the drums standing between them.

"Well...this one's a slow one, Luce," he says, in the voice he uses when Luce has been doing 'shrooms and doesn't remember exactly which planet he is on. Lucifer has repeating alien-themed highs. It's kind of creepy, actually. "But...I promise I'll work in space for a fucking killer drum solo next time, alright?"

Luce grins. "Fucking right," he answers.

"So, relax, right, Luce? Slow and no embellishments just yet," Dagen coaxes, and Doug and I pick up our instruments.

Dag counts us in. We've muddied through it at least a half dozen times tonight, yet the bridge still kind of does things to my feelings, even though I know it's just Dag knowing the business.

"And when will you get/that I need you to mean it," Dagen syncopates, utterly un-self-conscious, and fuck, he is unworldly in his element. It comes to a slow, melancholic end, and Dag looks satisfied. Less jittery than when we'd all arrived. And it feels good.

***

Dagen drives me home. Invites himself in.

"Do you have any booze?" Not waiting for a response, he flings open the cupboard above the fridge and smiles appreciatively at the selection. "Limes?" he requests.

I grab one from the fridge. I anticipated post-tour tequila night. This might have only been our second tour, but tequila has always been Dag's celebratory drink of choice.

"We're getting hammered," he informs me.

He pours us both a shot. And so it begins. Salt, shot, citrus, repeat.

I didn't cut enough lime slices for the amount of drinking that Dagen wants to do. I go for more, careful not to cut my fingers since I'm already feeling it.

"The thing about substance use," drunk-philosopher Dagen expounds, "is it's, like, at least seventy-three percent in your head."

"I bet that statistic is well-sourced," I reply, sarcastically. Dagen graciously ignores me.

"You have to be in the mood to be drunk. Are you in the mood to be drunk, Benjamin?"

"Sure, Dag." I brush him of in favour of lime slicing.

"Alright. Proof's in the pudding. Or in this case, in the tequila. I'm gonna line us up three shots, right? And you are going to demonstrate your dedication to the drunk by drinking them to me. With me. Ugh. Words. Drunk."

"I'm already drinking with you."

"Yes, but are you getting drunk with me?"

"I have little to no idea what you are talking about."

He claps me on the back. "Just go with it." He pulls out more shot glasses from the narrow cupboard beside the microwave and meticulously lines them up. The amber liquid looks kind of nice on the black granite counters, I think. "You need better shot glasses," Dagen advises me. "These are too classy. Shot glasses are not meant to be classy. These look like they came from Amara."

"They did come from Amara."

"That's your problem, right there. Next tour, we're buying you real shot glasses. Shot glasses with character, with pictures of sea animals, or the world's largest pizza or terrible puns or something. Something neon. Every town a new shot glass," he vows.

"Those won't look nearly as nice with my countertops," I inform him.

Dagen laughs. "Benji. I love you, but you are really fucking weird, you know that?"

"Or do you love me because I'm fucking weird?" I challenge.

"Both, prolly." He squeezes my shoulder with drunk affection. "Now, come on. Salt your hand, hold the lime, first shot. Other hand, another lime, another shot. While you're doing the second shot, I'll prime your first hand for the third shot, capisce?"

"So, it is basically just like every shot we've done so far tonight?" I clarify.

"Yeah," Dag agrees, "except faster!"

I nod amiably and salt both hands below the base of my thumb and tuck a lime crescent between each thumb and forefinger.

"Ready, steady, GO!" Dagen exclaims.

I lick my hand, down the first shot, suck a lime and repeat.

Dagen grabs my free hand, licks a stripe over the skin and sprinkles it with salt. "Go, go, go!" he chants.

I lick the salt up, licking where he licked, wondering if that should feel as intimate at it does. I drown out the pathetic, insidious thought with the final shot, and Dagen slips the last lime between my teeth.

Dagen whoops and pours himself three. I toss the sucked lime into the sink.

"Now you do me," he demands.

"Do you ever listen to the words that come out of your mouth?" I ask him.

"Only when I'm on the radio." He grins, cockily, and downs the first shot and begins on the second. He waves his hand in front of me, and I get what I'm supposed to do, but I freeze for a second. Dagen's having none of my hesitancy and practically smacks the back of his hand into my lips as he tips back his head to swallow his second shot. I quickly lick and salt his hand. He just tastes like salt from his previous shots. I don't know what I expected—something else? Something more? In a few seconds, his tongue laps over the skin where mine just was and he grins at me, swallowing the last of his tequila. I watch his throat, but then he's screeching at me, "Lime! Jesus, Ben, lime!"

I scramble and grab the wedge of the counter and offer it to him. I mean for him to grab it himself, but he just ducks his head and takes it, along with my fingertips. I quickly pull back and wipe my hands off on a dish towel.

Dagen's eyes are closed as if with pleasure as he sucks hard on the lime.

"There!" he pronounces, after he's gotten most of the juice, and drops the slice back onto the cutting board. "Now we are well en route to being drunk-bonded."

"I'm pretty sure drunk-bonded isn't a thing."

"It probably is in Valhalla," he argues.

***

37

Somehow we end up on the couch, blurrily playing Dr. Mario and munching on my mom's leftovers.

"Wanna know what I did last night?" Dagen asks, and I know that tone. Undoubtedly another fucking orgy with beautiful people with self-bestowed names like Ajaxx or Ryver or some shit. I'm suddenly not in the mood to humour him.

"Doubt it," is all I give him, and I delete a row of blues, thumb jamming into the button too violently because maybe I'm done with his never-ending need for commendation.

"Well, fuck you very much, too. Jesus."

I shove him with my shoulder, gently, trying to ease us back into comrade territory. "Just play the game."

He flings the control on the carpet childishly and stands, a sneer marring his face. It's an expression I've seen often enough, but it is rarely levelled at me.

He mutters something that ends in a bitter "fuck you" and then wobbles his way to the bathroom. The door is open and I hear the sound of him pissing. Then he groans and there's a choking sound as I realize he's puking.

I stay slouched against the cushions watching the screen, Dag's spitting and the sloshing of toilet water superimposed over the electronic notes. He doesn't come back, so eventually I stand—not so solid myself—and go to him.

I lean against the doorframe and see Dagen peering wistfully into the toilet.

"I just ate that asparagus." he mumbles, sadly.

I manage to pick my way across the bathroom and perch on the side of the tub. I reach over him, flushing the toilet. He makes a pained noise and presses his face into my knee. I let myself swat my knuckles chidingly against his skull before awkwardly unraveling a swath of TP and handing it to him.

He swipes at his mouth and sighs. He's quiet for a long minute and I wonder if he's gonna pass out. Instead, he uses my knees to stand himself up. "I should go." He mutters, a look of alcohol-induced determination imprinted on his face. He then teeters before sloping back down, catching himself jerkily on the edge of the bathtub.

"Don't be an idiot. You can't go anywhere now."

"Why not?" he retaliates.

"Because you're fucking drunk!"

"So are you."

"I'm not planning on going anywhere!"

He huffs, but stays put. He doesn't look well. His eyes are watery, and he's kind of pasty. We're both drunk as fuck. I slide onto the floor next to him, my body perpendicular to his, and collapse my forehead onto his shoulder. The tips of his fingers fiddle with my hair, shaggy over the back of my neck.

"Can we go to sleep, Benji?" he asks quietly. I nod. Slowly, on just this side of vertigo, we make it to my bedroom and collapse on the mattress. He's out almost immediately. I close my eyes and wait for the spinning to stop, but it doesn't.

***

I crawl out of bed late the next afternoon to find Dagen using my toothbrush. He has fair-trade coffee brewing in my kitchen, and apparently no plans of leaving anytime soon.

I feel that I should protest for the blatant disregard of my dental hygiene, but I'm too fucking hungover. I piss standing next to him with thoughts of retribution, but it doesn't bother him in the slightest. Stuff like that never does. Born shameless.

I wash my hands and he scrutinizes his face in the mirror.

"You gonna make me some French toast?" he asks.

"You want French toast?"

"Yeah."

Might as well.

We eat in hungover silence. I do the dishes. He surfs the net, playing songs for about twenty-five seconds before getting bored of them and starting something new. When I'm done, I sit on the couch next to him. He immediately closes the laptop and links his fingers carefully in his lap.

"So…are we going to, like, talk?" he asks.

"Talk about what?" I feel myself staring at him, completely nonplussed, but my insides twinge nervously regardless.

"What we started last night."

My eyes go round like a cartoon character's, and my eyebrows shoot up.

"Refresh my memory?" I play it safe.

"When we fucked?" he says, matter-of-fact.

I freeze, terror spreading to parts I can't even name.

Dagen brays. "A joke. Jesus," he manages to get out through his hysterics. "You should see your face! Beautiful." He collapses back on the couch, hooting to himself. I can't join in. My heart is beating as sporadically as a kid on a xylophone.

"Asshole," I mutter uselessly, but I doubt Dagen even hears me, too busy revelling in my panic.

"Oh, come on, Benji, I'm just joking you."

"Don't call me that!" I flare.

"Fine, sorry, Ben…" He's only pacifying me. He'll be back to Benji in minutes. "But, seriously, can we talk about it?"

"Seriously, I don't know what the fuck you're talking about."

"Last night. When I told you about getting laid, and you said you didn't care…and I want to know why you don't."

"Why I don't?" I echo.

"Give a fuck."

My eyebrows crease. "Um. Are you serious right now?"

"What? Yes, I'm fucking serious. I want to know why my best and fucking only friend in the whole fucking world doesn't care about my fucking life!"

I can't help but smile a little, and I know that makes him fume. "Dagen, calm down. Don't be so dramatic. And try to fit a few more 'fucking's in there, would you?"

He stews. I sigh.

"I do care about what happens in your life, Dag. You know that."

He grunts in disagreement.

"Dag, look. How many people have you slept with?"

"Hundred and forty eight." He fails at suppressing his smugness.

"See my point yet?"

He shakes his head deliberately.

I mull it over for a minute. "Okay, look. For you...having sex is like...masturbating. I mean, it feels good, but it doesn't have a heck of a lot of relevance to your life. It would be like...me telling you about every time I empty my compost bucket—something I do a lot that is not necessarily interesting to others. Do you get what I mean?" I take a breath. "It's like...you tell me you met someone, you're into someone, that's new. That's cool. I'm into it, I want to know..." Oh my god, I am so lying, but I plow right on. "You're hurt, you're pissed, you did something new, I wanna know. But fucking? I just can't bring myself to care because, like, it's boring. You've done it all. There is no new information to relate. I'm not trying to be an asshole, but does that, like, kinda make sense?"

"Fine," he says. "Yeah. Okay. Sorry."

His arms are crossed, though.

"Are you still mad at me?" I ask.

"No," he says in that way that means yes.

I slump my skull against the back of the couch, because seriously.

"Fuck, Dagen, can you just tell me what the problem is?"

"Me? I don't have a fucking problem," he says, like I do.

And he leaves. It's like being hung up on. And I made him fucking French toast and everything.

Chapter Five

I CATCH THE MONORAIL and transfer to a bus to get to the campus. My application was accepted, and I am officially registered for a psychology course and an art history course for no good reason except that they weren't too early in the morning. I hit up the bookstore to buy my textbooks and then head back towards home, stopping on the way to pick up some bacon and apples.

I'm bored. I thumb through my books and I fuck around online for a few hours, trying to get into some new tunes on Pandora, but I can't focus. And so, still groggy from the night before, I go to bed. Nothing better to do.

When the phone rings at exactly ten o'clock the next morning, I don't bother to open my eyes. I just assume it is Dagen calling to remind me that he's bored, as usual.

"Gonna say you're sorry, dickhead?" I answer with.

"Uh...Benjamin?"

Shit! I jump up and look at the cover of my phone but I don't know the number. "Um...hello? Sorry, who is this?"

"Uh, it's, um. It's me, actually." There's a small, extremely awkward pause. "Um. Lillian."

That would explain the ten o'clock thing. When we were dating, Lillian would always let me sleep in until exactly ten o'clock any day that we were going to hang out and didn't have school. It was like she was "allowing" me to sleep in, but then my time was her time. Just one more little annoyance in a clusterfuck of problems.

Weird hearing her voice, though; Lillian hasn't made an effort to contact me since…well, since we ended things.

"Lils?" I'm startled. God, her voice takes me back there, "I mean, uh, Lillian…"

"You can still call me that…or, whatever. Um." She tries. "I know this is probably kind of weird of me to call, considering… everything."

"No…it's cool, how…?"

"Your parents gave me your number."

"They always liked you."

"I'm sorry. This is awkward. I…I just wanted to talk to you. Could you, or…would you meet me for coffee sometime? Today, maybe? If you're not…um. Please?"

Okay. Officially bewildered here. "Yeah, of course I would. And today's good. Today's fine. When's good?"

***

So. I'm sitting across a table from my ex-wife at Sonnet, a nauseatingly bohemian café we used to frequent when we were dating. She looks different. It's been a year and a half; I guess I shouldn't be surprised. The blonde streaks are gone from her hair, which is all brown now, and her part has moved from the right to the left. It's longer, fanning out from her face in micro-ringlets. She looks pretty. Older in a good way.

We hugged awkwardly in the foyer. I ordered her a chai latte.

"You remembered," she says, sipping her drink.

"Huh?"

"The chai." She smiles.

"I spent half my paychecks on those things. Of course I remembered."

"Oh, God, I was so high maintenance." She laughs lightly.

We're falling easily into this. I remember how we were compatible, once, before.

I study her face. Her eyebrow piercing is gone. Same with the black eyeliner. Guess we've kind of changed places.

"Meh, I kind of liked it."

"Ben the Provider. Provider Ben," she says with a serious smile.

"They should make a movie." I shrug, a little uncomfortable with the praise.

"Totally."

I smile. At her. It's been a while. "So…how've you been?"

"Um… Not the absolute best, to be completely honest." Her voice is quiet and calm. "But things are…better. Getting there. I'm trying to…you know. Grow up."

I don't know wholly what she means, but I do a little bit, and she gives me an understanding, guilty sort of look.

"Uh, I guess that's kind of why I wanted to talk to you."

I don't say anything because I don't know what to say.

"Ben, I…I should have told you this before…but the pregnancy…"

"You. Um. Ended it."

Her eyes go round. "You knew?"

"You have a girlfriend pick you up, when you come home you're really sick—won't even let me come near you—and two days later you've miscarried? I might have been a fairly crappy boyfriend—and husband, for that matter—but I'm not stupid. Not completely."

She looks relieved. "No, you're not. And you weren't. Crappy, I mean. You were good. We just weren't. I had this idea of a what a relationship was, that was totally based on…I don't know. TV, and what my friends said, and what I read in shitty teen books, and not based on, like, us as people. Plus, we were teenagers—I guess we still are now, but it doesn't feel as awful, because being a teenager is kind of the actual worst, you know?"

I smile a little and nod. "Yeah. It really is."

We lapse into temporary silence, but it is not as awkward as before.

Lillian's eyes are on me, waiting.

"I hope…you weren't anxious about how I would react?" I try cautiously. "I mean, is it callous and assholey of me to say I was kind of relieved?"

"No," she says. "You were so careful to not bring it up, and that was really awesome of you, but…I kind of wanted you to. I mean, I absolutely don't blame you for not saying anything, I would've bitten your head off. But I didn't want the burden of having made the decision on my own.

"And then there is all the other stuff, like, for a while I…I thought I might have made a mistake. Afterwards. Like, maybe I wanted it after all. Well, I didn't want it. I didn't want that life. And I wanted to tell you, I did. But you hadn't even suggested it, so I half convinced myself that maybe you did want a baby, or at least you wanted to try being a father, and I just couldn't…and so maybe I was going to be breaking your heart, so then I was just sorry.

"I've been feeling guilty for too long now. Like, I know it was my decision and I don't owe it to you to tell you, necessarily, but I'm starting to move on with things, but I just felt you should know. That it was just as much your baby as mine, and I know that." She breathes out, her cheeks puffing out adorably for a moment, and I feel a pang of something.

I clumsily reach for her hand, and she lets me.

"Lils…we'll never know, right? If it was the right call? I mean, it probably was. So why don't we just say that? You made the right call, and you're happy now, right?"

She nods. "Yeah, I am. I'm editing this 'zine, and I'm seeing this guy, and I think my parents have finally forgiven me, and everything is just falling into place again."

"That's good, Lils, that's really awesome. I'm happy for you." I am, and that feels good, but it hurts.

She's crying a little. I've made her cry, yet again. But I don't feel guilty about it because she's squeezing my hand.

"Oh, fuck, Ben. You were always good at the comforting thing." She composes herself quickly, dabbing at her eyes with a compostable napkin. "So...how about you? Dating anyone?"

"I... Nope. Not really. Busy with the band and stuff."

She laughs. "Well, yeah. God. I see you on TV all the time and, like, people wearing Allusion shirts, and... It is *so* weird. I remember going to your shows and being so proud of being, like, the girlfriend of one of the guys in the band. But, God, Ben, it is so cool. Like, I am wicked proud of you."

We finish our drinks, and she asks if I want to take a walk in the park. I find that I do. She wraps a vivid purple pashmina around her neck.

"I'm glad you called," I say, quite honestly, after a while, our boots leaving footprints in the shallow springtime mud.

"I'm glad I called, too." She smiles.

"I kind of thought that this was closed forever."

"Yeah, well, with distance and time and everything, remembering stuff with you doesn't seem so...intimidating. You know, I blamed you."

"For the pregnancy thing?"

"That, and for the not-breaking-up-with-me thing. You should've. I should've. We both knew it was supposed to end, but we didn't how to do it."

"That's... That's pretty much exactly it. How come I could never phrase it like that?"

Lillian just smiles.

"So...tell me about this new guy." I veer away from all this serious talk.

"Uh, his name is Radley. He's twenty-two, and he's in my postcolonial history class at school—did I tell you I'm back at school?"

"No, you didn't. That's rad. At U-Dub?"

"Yeah." She smiles.

"Cool. You and, uh, Radley. Is it serious?"

"Honestly? No, not really. Which is why it's so nice. How the hell did we end up so serious so fast?"

"I have no fucking clue, but I was left pretty damn surprised by it," I say, shaking my head.

"Ha. Me, too. Honestly, marriage? How fucked up is that? So, tell me about Ms. Not Really," she says casually.

"Huh?"

"When I asked you if you had someone, you said not really, and I have had friends who are girls for almost twenty years now, and not to be totally gender essentialist, but when a girl says 'not really,' it means 'not a relationship-relationship but kinda-sorta *something*,' so spill, Walard-Walkens."

I laugh. "I think you're over-analyzing, there, Paresky."

"And I think I'm onto something!" she teases.

I clam up, stupid, and maybe blushing.

"C'mon, Ben, we were doing so well, considering we haven't spoken, for, like, ever."

I pause. Might as well say it to her if I'm going to say it to anyone. Since we're heart-to-hearting and all.

"Look there is…someone."

"Okay, and she…?" She looks at me carefully.

"Um." I bite my lip and look at my boots.

"Oh!" There it is. A short surprised syllable. "Shit." She says quickly. "Sorry. Fuck. Sorry. Should not have assumed. Sorry. I mean, that's totally cool. I just. Didn't see…that one coming."

I exhale slowly, and the realization that I've actually said it out loud before I've even admitted it to myself kind of hits me. "Jesus, I can't believe—no one knows," I confess.

"Yeah?" she asks. "Have you not…come out to anyone?"

"Come out?" I look at her blankly for a long, stupid moment. Oh. Yeah. I guess that is what this is. "I never really thought about it like that."

"Um. Yeah, shit. Sorry. Again with the assuming. So. Not gay. Just…bi? Curious? Bi-curious? Pan? Fuck. Sorry again. You don't need to identify as anything. It is none of my fucking business I just..."

I laugh, "It's okay. Identifying or whatever isn't going to come up, because nothing is going to happen, and nothing *has* happened. There's just this guy. And I just have these... stupid feelings. And nothing is going to come of them. And on top of that, I've actually only ever slept with women, so even if something *were* to happen, I wouldn't even know how. God. You did not want to know that."

"Oh, I absolutely did." She grins, "I mean, I wasn't going to pry. Okay, that is bullshit. I was absolutely going to pry, but I was going to be as sneaky and tactful about it as possible."

I push my shoulder playfully into hers, and suddenly it's like tenth grade again, before we were dating. Before things got so brutally intense. When Lillian and I were friends, and when we'd go what she termed "adventuring," which usually involved stupid-fun shit like garage-saling and streetcar surfing and sneaking out at night just for the novelty of sneaking out at night.

"I can't believe you never told me." She laughs, and hits me on the arm. "Douche."

"Dildohead."

"Dild—oh my god, I am having the worst visual right now. Like instead of a head, just having a dildo? That is actually terrifying."

"But the real question is, what kind of dildo? Jelly pink? Vibrating with beads? Or the *FIST OF POWER?*"

"Oh my GOD." Lillian shrieks, but she's laughing, and I like it. "So, tell me about him!" she demands, once she's recovered

"What? Oh, God, no. Definitely not. Not gonna happen, sorry, Lils."

She looks like she's considering feeling hurt—I can see the dark freckles on her nose get caught in creases—and then suddenly her eyes go bright, "Oh, man, Benj, is he totally famous? That is so crazy. God, when you two finally get together and fall madly in love and take the media by storm, I will be like, 'Oh, yeah, that is my ex-husband, sort-of-gay-emo-punk-rocker, no big deal.'"

I shake my head without any real exasperation. "Shut up. Nothing will probably come of it anyway."

"Well…I'm rooting for you."

"Well, thanks, Paresky."

Still smiling, she links her arm with mine. "I'm meeting The Boy in an hour. But you can walk me home if you like."

"And what if I have things to do?" I tease.

"You don't have a job. You don't have things to do."

"I have a job…" I protest weakly.

"It's your off season."

I can't really argue with that. "So, does this mean we're friends, then?"

"Obviously."

"Okay, cool. Um, Lils?"

"You haven't told anyone about this, and I need to keep my mouth shut or suffer the consequences?"

"Yeah. Pretty much. Except, it will be me who's suffering the consequences, and I know all about your soft spot for compassion, so I'm trusting you."

"Done deal, sailor." She hums a couple of bars of "In the Navy."

"Oh, fuck off."

At her door, I hug her. Looking down the few inches to her eyes is just so familiar that it just slips out. "I love you." I freeze. "Shit. Sorry. I'm pretty sure that that was situational…"

She laughs. "Don't be a douche. I love you, too. Like, that never stopped, just changed."

I relax. "Yeah. That way. Whatever the fuck that means."

She smiles for the millionth time and—and, fuck, it's just so fucking good to see her smiling. While we were married…well. I didn't see a lot of it.

"See ya later, Benjamin. Thanks for the chai."

"Yeah. Talk to you soon. Call me, you know?"

"Will do."

Chapter Six

I GIVE DAGEN A couple of days. He's consistently more stubborn than me, however, and when he doesn't show, I figure I might as well go to him. I don't have that whole oh-but-that's-giving-in complex; it's not really in my nature. So, the next day, I show up at Miranda's.

"Benjamin!" She's happy to see me. She's a friendly person; she's happy to see everyone. I give her a hug. She holds my face between her two small hands, scrutinizing my chi or something, probably, before planting a lip-balmy kiss on my cheek. "How are you, honey? You look beautiful!"

I smile. I've been greeted this way at Dagen's for literally years.

We do the regular small-talk thing. Her flitting around, showing off the myriad of tacky, angel-themed kitsch that litter her dusty hallway shelves, me nodding and offering awkward admiration.

"Dagen around?" I ask after I've made what I think is a reasonable amount of appreciative noise.

"In the basement, hun. Been there for days. You'd think with the money you boys are making he'd finally move out. But he goes on about how he's saving to buy me a new house, you know. That's my darling boy!" She looks misty eyed for a moment before her face splits wide with a grin. "Well, you both are!" She crushes me into another hug before shooing me downstairs.

I guiltily admit that I am a little surprised. I thought Dagen was saving to buy himself a grotesquely expensive car or his very own recording studio or something. Go figure.

The stairs are still wobbly, and creak even more than they did when I was a kid. I was afraid of them back then and always tried to talk Dagen out of going to the basement. The lack of banister made me nervous, as did the part where they weren't carpeted: just rickety two-by-fours with multiple crayon drawings of blue whales, courtesy of a much younger Dagen.

It stinks. Dagen is lying on the ancient hide-a-bed, his feet sticking out the end of the completely unzipped sleeping bag he's used as a blanket for as long as I can remember. The bottom corner is flipped up; sky with oddly proportioned hockey players skating decorate the cotton lining. I used to be so jealous of that sleeping bag. I thought it would make every night like camping. The rest of Dagen presents as a long, thin lump under shiny fabric.

I lift the top edge of the sleeping bag very carefully, just exposing the top of his head, and my target, his ear. I bring my mouth close.

"Dagen..." I whisper.

No response.

"Dag..." A little louder.

He groans unhappily, rolls over, exposing his other ear.

"Dagen. Wake the fuck up."

He cracks an eye open, glaring dangerously. He looks vaguely confused.

"Benji?"

"Mm. Heard you were devolving into an invertebrate," I tell him, straightening up.

He sits up, scratching himself unattractively. "Thought it would prove an interesting experiment." His voice is crackly with morning.

He gets out of bed and heads over to the corner, where he's installed a shitty little bathroom with not-quite-ceiling-height walls and no door. As he showers, we banter easily and I pack up the hide-a-bed, folding his sleeping bag and draping it over the cushions.

Of course, when Dagen reappears he's naked.

Luckily, I am pretty used to his thoughtless displays of nudity and manage not to embarrass myself by blushing or staring or even acting too uncomfortably. He steps, commando, into some jeans, but doesn't bother with a shirt and sits next to me. I've already turned on the Xbox. We play brainlessly for a while when all of the sudden he stops.

"Hey!" he says, and at first I think he's just whiny because he keeps dying. But I realize he's said it like he just had some revelation. "Hey, aren't I mad at you?"

"What?"

"If I wasn't mad at you, there is no way I would even be here. I'd be waking up on your fucking couch. I never stay at home."

"You're not mad at me! Remember, I even asked and you said no!"

"Yeah, but I said it in that way that you'd know I still was!"

"Dag, you're not really supposed to disclose that. It's supposed to be implied," I instruct, purposefully being a patronizing asshole. "Now that you've said it, you've pretty much wrecked the whole delivery."

"Fuck off, Benji," he says, shoving me. He's not mad. It looks like he's trying but can't quite remember the moment enough to reanimate the grudge.

I throw down my controller and stretch.

"Neither of us even know what you were mad about, so what does it matter? God, it fucking stinks in here. You hungry? Let's get breakfast."

He seems in agreement and pulls on a shirt and cracks the window above the bed that has a stunning view of the gravel under the deck. He turns back to the room, catches my eye, and smiles.

And just like that, we're back to how we always are. It reassures me, but I still can't shake the feeling of gnawing disappointment. It was stupid of me to even think about this, ever. We're best friends. That shit he pulled on the road was just him being bored and fucking with me. And now we are home and things are cool, and whatever it all was is done and over with. I force myself to believe it.

***

So Dagen decides we need to go clubbing. I have to put on a tight shirt and studded belt and a leather cuff and everything. Dagen believes that the number one single best thing about our profession is the ability to purchase really, really good fake IDs, and that we need to take advantage of these IDs often.

We head out to Immersion, a trendy club downtown, where Dagen says "the energy is good." What he means is people there recognize him and he gets free drinks. Typically, the free drinks extend by proxy to me, so I can't exactly complain.

He's not wrong. The DJ is on point, and there are lots of girls wearing a whole lot of not much, so things are cool. With Dagen somewhere beside me, scoping the floor for a partner, I find myself dancing with a lithe black girl. She's slightly tipsy and has a sparkly top, and my libido is admittedly interested. She doesn't recognize me and I prefer that. Her body feels warm and fluid under my hands. We converse sporadically, and I don't mind at all when she presses closer, her palm sliding along my ribs to my back, her hips rolling, intent and inviting, and everything is casual and nice and—

"Uh, hey, uh...aren't you guys from the Allusion?" A voice calls out, loud enough to be heard over the pounding music. Taken off guard, I turn around to find a young-but-balding white guy with four girls clustered around him, faces a spectrum of emotions from excited to guilty-embarrassed. He has obviously been delegated with the task of asking.

I attempt to go for the old *I don't know what you're talking about* look. But I know that is just wishful thinking on my part with Dagen around.

"Why yes, yes we are." Dagen grins wolfishly.

I flash a guilty smile at the girl I was dancing with, and she looks back at me vaguely stunned. She tilts her head, questioning, and I shrug: a silent conversation.

And so we end up, under Dagen's careful publicity-aware eye, clustered together with a bunch of gawking people who are madly talking and taking what can only be grainy, dark pictures on various flip phones.

Dagen is happily chatting everyone up and signing autographs and all that shit. I attempt to follow suit but I'll never have his easy confidence. I'm vaguely useless at this whole fame thing. Soon enough, one girl pulls out an actual camera, asking for photos. She squeezes between us, posing with her cheeks sucked in and her chin tilted unnaturally. She checks the camera and makes the guy pressing the button take, like, ten more before she is satisfied.

"Can I have one of just you two?" she asks, and I obligingly stand next to Dagen. Without warning, though, he's got me caught. Standing behind me with one splayed hand pressing hard into my abs, his elbow jutting out angularly, and his other hand gripping my hair, yanking my head back far enough to expose my neck. Suddenly his teeth are poised over my pounding carotid. He shoves a leg between mine, connecting us calf to calf and thigh to thigh. I can just picture him, teeth down, startling eyes staring intensely at the camera. It clicks, flashes, and then he drops me, casually, smirking.

"That was actually super hot!" one of the girls declares drunkenly, and within a minute, there are, like, six other girls wielding phones and begging us to stay put.

Dagen pulls me closer, planting himself more firmly behind me. I feel a patch of not-quite-cool air on the skin of my low back where Dagen is slowly rucking it up with self-assured fingers. I make a slight noise in protest, and he replies with a shushing noise against my neck. His hand is under my shirt now, his hot, deliberate fingers tracing the line just above where my jeans start, teasing, daring me to react, all while knowing I won't do a goddamn thing.

The phones and cameras are eventually all put away, and he releases my hair and relaxes his posture but his hand doesn't leave its new, hidden residence beneath my shirt. The small circle of enthusiastic fans crowds closer as he chats away. Their view of him is partially obscured by my body, and he's congenially answering all their questions, telling them to add us online. That we'd love to hear from them.

"Right, Ben?"

I jump. All my efforts have been focused on not betraying on my face the feeling of his clever hand pressing into the muscles alongside my vertebrae; on pretending not to notice the electrically charged spirals being etched into my skin by his possessive fingertips.

"Yeah," I answer, articulately.

"He's shy," Dag tells them, and I blush, not so much because the girls are looking at me with that isn't-that-adorable? gaze, but more because Dagen's spread open his hand and laid it over my spine, stroking, sending jolts of *something* up my backbone. It's all I can do not to let my breath hitch.

"So, how do you ladies fill your time?" Dagen continues, as if he's actually interested. I think I can say with accuracy that's he's not. Not nearly as interested in them as he is in the mental fucking anguish he's causing me.

"Uh, well, Sam and I are in college," a girl with an impressive rack informs me. Admittedly, I would probably be more interested in looking at it if Dagen wasn't otherwise distracting me. "I'm in engineering, and she's in art history."

"You don't say." Dagen grins, brushing a knuckle along one of my lower ribs, not going any great distance but commanding every particle of concentration that I have. "Benjamin just signed up for an art history course for September."

"No way! That is so cool! At SSCC?" she demands.

I manage to nod.

"Me, too! Which one?"

Fuck. Why did I even mention that to Dagen? Never again. I'm never telling him anything. Ever. Again.

"Yeah, what was it again, Ben?" he asks, his hand skimming to my side and squeezing, dangerously close to some fans' sight lines. I almost react. Almost push him off me, but then Dagen would have his victory, and if Dagen has that...will he stop?

I hate myself. I really, really do. Because I can't do it. I can't let this end. The club is just dark enough to hide the shape of his hand as he eases his palm up and down, and his stupid hand on my stupid skin is all I fucking want.

"Uh, 111." I manage. "Survey of Western Art or something?"

"Oh, yeah, that's a decent course." She nods, eagerly. "Just make sure you don't have Phillips. I hear she's a total hardass."

"Yeah, I don't think that sounds familiar."

"Cool. Well, maybe I'll see you around on campus, then." She smiles. And that's nice. It really is, and I really wish I could concentrate on how she's nice and how it would be just fine to see her around, or even get to touch her, but now Dagen, the fucker, is securing a grip at the back of my jeans, his fingers dipping just below the edge, and creeping toward my tailbone. The girls seem to be a bit jittery, with booze or excitement.

"We're going to go dance for a bit," one of them states boldly, implying that maybe we would like to join them.

Dagen smiles smoothly at them. "Alright. It was really cool to meet you guys."

"You, too. And thanks for the photos."

"Anytime."

And they're gone. I whirl around, glaring at him furiously.

"What the *fuck* was that, Dagen?" I ask, my jaw clenching.

"Just checking for lumps," he says, smiling innocently.

"I hate you. You know that, right? Absolutely fucking *hate* you."

"Yes, I could tell that by the way you grabbed my hand and said, 'Stop that right now, Dagen Mercutio Brown!' Oh, wait. You didn't do that. Don't you think that's weird, Benji?"

"Screw you."

He flashes his teeth at me. "Oh, come on, I was just fucking with you."

"You're always just fucking with me."

"And yet never fucking you. Which is odd, because fucking with and then fucking is my usual progression." I blush, and he grins. "Come on, Benj...I was just having some fun."

"Okay. Fine. Whatever. Are we going to dance?"

"Wouldn't want to keep the fans waiting."

"Whore."

"Tease."

"Fucker."

"Got me there." He smirks and grabs my arm. I find the nice art history student and we dance.

At the end of the night, I don't ask for her number.

Chapter Seven

W HAT DO YOU mean, you're hanging out with Lillian?"
Dagen, having woken up this morning on my couch,
obviously symbolizing his no longer being angry at me, is now
angry at me. He hates Lillian. I thought it was a jealous *Oh, no!
You're cutting back on my Benjamin time!* high school thing, but
apparently, I was wrong. Because Dagen sure isn't looking too
happily at the Belgian waffles I unthawed solely for him. I swear
he would never get breakfast if it weren't for me.

"I mean that she called me about an hour ago and asked what
I was up to, and I said not a lot, so we're going to head out to the
mall or the park or something."

"Oh. Well, gee whiz, don't I feel foolish?" he spits.

"What?"

"Didn't know I was out of the Benjamin loop."

"Christ, Dag, You're not." I try to placate him.

"Well, Benjamin, if you were going to start seeing your ex-wife
again, I just thought you would have told me. You know. Your
best friend?"

"You are so not pulling a guilt trip on me, you douchebag,
so don't even try it. And we're not *seeing* each other. We're just
hanging out, *and* she has a boyfriend, so fucking relax already."

"Not seeing each other," he repeats. "Right. So it's just a get-
together, remember-old-times, *oh wasn't it funny when you
ruined my life you stupid bitch* friends thing."

"Lillian didn't ruin my life, Dagen."

"Seems that way to me."

"It always fucking seemed that way to you. I don't even know what your problem was with her. And I sure as hell thought you'd be over it by now."

"She was fucking controlling, that's all. I don't see why you're going to bother wasting your time with her again."

I shake my head with frustration. He's so fucking stubborn sometimes. "We get along, Dagen. We used to, and it turns out we still do. So get the fuck over it."

"Fine. Over it," he says, so obviously not. "When did you start seeing her again, anyway."

"Last week. She called me up and we went for coffee and talked about…everything."

"Everything?" His voice is sharp.

"Like…she finally admitted it was an abortion and shit, and we talked about her, like, feelings about that and stuff."

"Right."

"Yeah… Look, Dag, what's going on? This is an unusual amount of dramatics, even for you."

"I'm good," he insists. "Thought I'd call up Doug today, anyway."

"You never call up Doug. Nobody calls up Doug. Doug doesn't talk. You have to just hope he's listening."

"Well…" He sounds a little lost for excuses.

"Look, do you wanna just chill here for the day? Then we can jam for a bit when I get home."

"Yeah. Okay." He doesn't look at me.

"Alright. So…I'll talk to you late?"

"Yeah. Fine." Fuck, he's so tiring sometimes.

"Okay. Good."

"Thanks for the waffles," he mutters, still sullen, but not as bad.

"You're welcome."

***

"Here. I've written something. Just a chorus," is the first thing Dagen says to me when I get home.

I read the lines. "Has it got music?"

He nods. "Some."

He grabs my acoustic, which he has dug out of my room, and fucks around with a few chords for a bit, but eventually plays it for me. I love getting to hear it first. Which is kind of lame, I know, because I'm in the band, so, like, of course I get to hear it first. Hell, if it's trash, I'm the *only* one who gets to hear it. But still, the idea of a little piece of music put together for the first time and coupled with lyrics that haven't ever been written all coming spilling out of Dagen's talented mind... It's neat, is all.

"Because it was midnight/then it was two a.m./and we were parked beside the bridge/looking down at the stars/because you always had a thing for reflections."

He looks at me, waiting for approval that is easy to give.

"It's good," I say.

Dagen nods, seriously. He may fuck around about a lot of shit. But not with this.

"I don't have verses."

We'll figure something out."

We fiddle around with it for a good few hours.

"Try that bit again," Dagen instructs, and comes in with a rough first stanza. *"Somewhere you've misplaced your veins and heart and skin/pared back the biological, trying to focus in/on all we tried to make matter/but we're just mouth-to-mouth and limb-to-limb/I guess for you, vanity has never been a sin."*

He stops. "We need more words there. What have we got?"

I lean over our scrap of messy paper. "Where?"

"Between 'you' and 'vanity.' Carrying it for an extra note just sounds stupid and lazy."

He's standing close next to me, and my mind considers dwelling on that fact, but I find I can't. I'm pulled into this, too, making this thing together. "You mean like a name?"

"Maybe."

"Not generic? Like hun, babe, or whatever?"

"No, I don't think so."

I stare at the segment, play it over in my head. The fourth line is muted, so the last needs to be more bold.

"Maybe we don't need another word," I think out loud. "We could just change the spacing. Like, sharper on 'you' and a pause, and then that kind of high-pitch shouty, 'Against Me!'-ish thing you do for 'vanity' and another little pause, and then the rest of the line."

"Hm." He considers. "Could we try it?"

"Yeah, of course," I agree and come in with the chords.

"Was that better?" His black bangs fall in front of his eyes, and he does the stupid, endearing headshake thing. He's looking at me intently.

"I liked it," I offer. "Really."

"Good." He yawns. "Sweet. Speaking of two a.m.…."

"Are you kidding?" I look blearily at my phone. "Shit."

"We get into this, Benji. It's what we're good at." He's smiling at me kind of intently. I shake it off.

"Mm," I agree. "Bed?"

"Yeah."

***

"You need a fucking TV in your ceiling," Dagen mutters sleepily.

I grunt, as if considering the possibility. Dagen's been here three or four nights now. Sometimes on the couch, sometimes flopped beside me in bed, and to be honest, I'm used to him. I like him here. It's easy and keeps me from getting bored or lonely, but still. Makes me nervous that I'm getting too dependent or something.

"Don't you get sick of me?" I ask.

"Yep," he murmurs, one arm draped comfortably across his stomach, the other curled above his head.

"Liar." I give a lazy rebuttal.

"Mm. Maybe." He's asleep, the fucker. And on my side of the bed, too.

I kick off my jeans, tug off my shirt, crawl under the covers.

I wonder if it's weird that I could recognize Dagen's breathing anywhere.

***

Sometime later, before it's actually morning, I wake up. I try to remember what woke me, but I can't figure it out. I glance at Dagen and realize he's glancing at me at exactly the same time. It's kind of surreal; I could have sworn he was sleeping.

Now we're caught.

The casual glance somehow stuck, and I can't—or maybe I just won't—look away. I'm in that weird early-early-morning mood, the uninhibited, *say anything, we'll sleep it off later* feeling. But we're not speaking. He's just looking at me, not smiling or smirking or trying to make me laugh. Just looking, somewhere between emotionless and thoughtful. I think it's affecting my breathing.

I'm stretched out on my side, just like him, but I can't seem to focus on any part of my body besides my eyes. Or, more, his eyes. It's too dark to see them well. A little bit of pre-dawn light is tripping through the cracks around the thick, grey curtains, but not enough for real clarity. Not that I need it. Dagen's eyes are pretty damn familiar to me. Blue, in a *not trying that hard to be blue* sort of way. For Dagen, it's all in the lashes. They are pretty fucking beautiful. Not curled or anything, but there are lots of them—so many dark-brown lashes that sometimes you swear he's wearing makeup even when he's not. The shape hints at something not quite usual, and a little intriguing, if you stare at them long enough. Apparently.

It's been full minutes. I realize suddenly that it's not the shape or the color or the lashes that make Dagen's eyes so undeniably appealing. It's the certainty. Like he knows what he's going to do next, no matter what it is, it's going to be a good move on his part.

And suddenly he is doing something. Without me noticing, he has moved closer to me, close enough that I can feel the end traces of his breath hit my chin angularly. The backs of his fingers are on my cheek, so light I can only just differentiate between the knuckle and nail and air. He drags them down, slow over the slight hollow. I can't help it. I lick my lips and swallow, suddenly more aware of myself than I think I have ever been. I blink slowly and he kisses me. I think. I already don't know. It was just a brush of something over my lips. So light that I can't even tell if it happened or if I'm just making things up. Wishful thinking and all. I see his lips twitch in a slight smile, his hand gone from my face, he blinks and turns over. And he's asleep. And I wonder if maybe I am, too. I can't tell anymore.

***

I don't get the chance to analyze my dream-memory thing, though, because when I next wake up, it is to the shrill, electronic sound of my ringtone. It is almost four in the morning, and if anyone calls me at this time, it's Dag. And he's here, so... I reach bodily over Dagen to grab the phone that rests on the table next to my side of the bed.

"'Lo?" I can barely get sounds out, my voice is so useless.

"Ben? It's Luce. Uh. Fuck. Um. Something's happened."

I'm sitting, leaning against the headboard, Dagen looking concerned beside me.

Luce is prattling on so fast I can't even understand—that and my brain is already sticky as tree sap.

"Luce. Stop. What happened? Speak slowly."

Dagen's fully awake now. I look over at him, and his eyes are wide, worried, curious.

"It's Doug, man," Lucifer says, voice shrill and tense, and I know he's high. "We were just having some fun, but I think the shit we got was laced and…"

"Luce. What's wrong with him? Where are you?"

"We're at the hospital, uh, Northwest or something. Benj, I didn't know what to do. Is he gonna get in trouble from the cops? Fuck."

"How is he, Luce? Focus. Is he stabilized?"

"I don't know, man, I'm freaking out. He's in some unit, I can't remember which, too many fucking letters. Can you…"

"We'll be there in a few minutes, Lucifer. Now listen to me, okay? I need you to find a vending machine and get yourself a bottle of water. Then sit down, away from other people, if possible, and drink as much water as you can, and just try and calm down, okay, Luce? You're gonna be fine, and me and Dag will be there really soon, got it? And you call me, okay, if anything happens or you freak or whatever, you call me."

"Yeah. Yeah, okay, I'll…see you guys…" He sounds lost and scared.

I'm officially worried.

"We've gotta go," I say, grabbing my wallet and looking imploringly at Dagen, who's already standing. I'm feeling almost as freaked out as Lucifer was sounding. I start towards the door.

"Benji, it's gonna be fine. You have time to put your clothes on." Dagen's voice is soothing, but he's too nervous to actually tease me about the fact that I'm not wearing anything but boxers. Jesus, my head sometimes.

I'm shaking with adrenaline, or worry or something, but I manage to pull on some clothes in the dark. Dagen lays a hand on my shoulder, but I flinch away like it's some kind of offensive. I'm too frayed to be touched, can barely keep track of myself.

Dagen grabs his keys, and we're driving through the mainly empty streets. Dag throws me his phone.

"Call Abby. Tell her to meet us there."

As the phone rings, I realize it: Dagen is the one being calm and rational. Not me. If it were possible for me to be any more in shock than I already am, that might just put me over.

On my third try, Abby, Doug's twin sister, answers. I tell her what's going on, say I'm sorry we don't know more. She tells me gravely that she'll meet us at the hospital. I shove the phone in my pocket and stare out the window, my mind racing while I try to force my pulse to keep tempo.

"Hey, Benji, you okay? I need you to breathe slower, okay, bud?"

This can't be happening. Doug is a fucking horse. He can take anything; if something's got him sick…I look at Dagen with wide eyes. He smiles lightly. His hand touches my knee, and this time I don't flinch it off. He squeezes my knee for just a second.

"It's Doug, Benj. You really think there's a drug Doug can't handle?"

I know Dagen must be worried, too, but he seems so sure that I just look at him and nod.

"Exactly," Dagen agrees. "So can you take a deep breath for me, sugar, please?"

I do, shakily, and realize that Dagen was right; my breathing was off. I fill my lungs up again and again.

I can't really take it, but my mind is finally slowing down and I'm calming. I slump forward, cradling my head with my arms on the dash. Dagen reaches out and presses his palm against my back, soothing me with circles.

"It's okay, Benji, sweetness, we got this," I hear him say, almost absently, but not. If I were actually here, in this moment, I would be pretty much psyched right now.

Chapter Eight

MANAGING TO GET me somewhere in the realm of sane, Dagen parks, and we walk through the parking lot to the waiting room, his hand not leaving my lower back until we reach the automatic doors. Luce is sitting alone in the corner, one leg jittering with nervous energy, in one of those sketchy, metal mesh chairs. I grab a seat next to him, leaving Dagen to go try and figure out what the hell is going on.

"Hey, Luce," I greet carefully.

"Hey, man." He looks at me with shifty-blown pupils and red-rimmed irises. He's high as a fucking satellite.

"You doing alright?" I try to keep my voice calm, confident as Dagen was for me.

He looks distracted. "Oh, yeah. Fucking fine. This place is weird, though, don't you think?"

"Uh, yeah, I guess. You know. Hospitals."

I survey the room: fake flowers in old-lady-pink plastic vases on eighties-style wooden tables. The linoleum has chipped in places, exposing concrete. The people all look just plain tired.

I watch Dag at the counter, smiling easily with the receptionist as he fills out form after form. He tosses his head, his bangs swinging off his forehead for a moment before falling right back into place. The young woman behind the counter in forest-green scrubs watches his movements just as I do. I know I'm jealous in some ridiculous way. I've spent most of my life being jealous of the people Dagen chooses, however briefly his interest may last. I'm used to it, but that doesn't make it not hurt. And besides, I comfort myself, I wouldn't want him to be looking that way at me. Because that's not how Dagen really smiles.

Luce's head darts upwards from where he was watching his hands suspiciously to follow my line of sight.

"Ben?" he whispers, barely moving his mouth.

"Yeah?" I say, barely moving my eyes.

"When the fucking hell did Dagen get here?"

I smile, finally, relieved, because I thought he was gonna say something way stranger. "He came with me, Luce."

But he's not listening anymore, staring intently at a hotel-room-bland watercolour that hangs over his head as if it is a Magic Eye print.

"C'mon, c'mon, c'mon," he mutters.

Abby arrives. I wave her over, stand, and give her an awkward hug. We don't know each other all that well, but this is what people do, right?

"Dagen's taking care of the insurance and payments and stuff. Don't worry about it," I tell her.

She nods. Unlike Doug, she actually does speak, but I can tell that this is not exactly the time for a public forum. She looks terrible, her hair pulled messily back in an unplanned ponytail, so obviously having just been roused from bed.

I grab her a coffee from a vending machine.

"Thanks, Ben," she acknowledges and falls back into worried contemplation.

"I'm sure he'll be fine..." I try, but I don't have Dagen's confidence. Not even close.

"We don't know that," she answers grimly, then sets herself to ignore mode.

Dagen shakes his head, arches his back a bit in a stretch, scratches the back of his neck. The receptionist is staring at him shamelessly now. I see her roll her lips into her mouth and out again, contemplatively.

He's thanking her, turning, walking back over to us. Not grinning anymore.

He sits next to me.

"So?" I'm reluctant to hear, but I know I have to. Abby looks at him expectantly.

"He's stable."

"That's good, right?" I can't think.

"It's alright. They don't think he's going to die on us or anything."

Abby exhales in relief.

"Right." I sigh. All that adrenaline and now it's just leaking from my body, leaving me exhausted. I let my head fall backwards into the wall with a thud.

"So...what do we do?" I ask. I honestly don't know. Not a single possible plan of action will form in my mind.

"We can stay here, wait until morning, see if he's allowed visitors, or we can head out and get a bit of sleep and come back tomorrow."

"Oh." I guess I had pictured us camping out in Doug's room, one of us grabbing his arm, the other two looking concerned or some shit like that.

Luce is perched on his chair, his head twitching on his neck like a ruffled pigeon.

"We should get him home," I observe. "You okay?" I ask Abby. "We need to get Luce out of here before he causes a scene, but I can stay with you if you want?"

"No, don't worry about it. Our folks will be here soon, anyway. Thanks for everything, guys. I'll call you when he's allowed to see people, or whatever. If Mom doesn't kill him."

She manages a watery smile, and I echo it. "Alright." I nod. "You sure?"

"Yeah. I'm good. Thanks, though. We'll worry about Doug, and you guys can worry about Michael."

"Yeah." Dag nods and stands. "C'mon, Luce. We're gonna get out of here. Bye, Abby."

Luce ignores him but seems to comply when Dagen lightly grabs hold of his sleeve and directs him towards the door. Dagen gives the woman still standing at the counter a friendly wave.

"I think he's getting worse," I remark, eying Lucifer as he scuttles along behind us.

"They'd just taken them when he called. Doug had an allergic reaction."

"Not an overdose," I acknowledge. I knew Doug was a tank. "What was it, anyway?"

"'Shrooms with a bit of something else thrown in."

I nod.

Luce is staring at light in the parking lot as Dag unlocks his car.

"Holy shit..." Lucifer is quivering. "That thing's gonna go. It's gonna fucking blow our heads off."

"C'mon," Dagen says sternly, yanking Luce's arm and shoving him in the car. He doesn't have a lot of tolerance for loss of control, which is a bit ironic, considering his dramatics.

Guess he doesn't get that Luce doesn't even have control when he's sober. Sometimes I'm surprised that we've made it through two tours and Luce still has both his legs. Or, more, his voice box, because if Dagen had the choice, that would be the first to go.

Lucifer makes guttural, stuttering sounds in his throat, and Dagen angrily flicks his keys on the ignition and hits on his lights. I crawl into the back to buckle Lucifer in.

"Living things are everywhere," Lucifer tells me, though I'm fairly certain he's not actually talking to me.

"They sure are, Luce," I agree. Dagen glares at us in the rearview mirror, but I just shrug.

"My body is an ant colony," he continues. I watch Lucifer trace his wrist's veins with his finger curiously. "The queen lives... here." He indicates a vein in his palm. His voice is bland.

"*Fucking bitch!*" he screeches suddenly. "*Get the fuck out of my hand!*" Suddenly, he assaults his hand with his fingernails, trying to dislodge the imaginary insect from his skin. He draws blood before I manage to grab his hand and suppress him.

"Get him to shut the fuck up!" Dagen yells at me, the stress of the evening obviously getting to him, now that I don't need to be looked after.

"Shh, Luce, hey, it's okay." I pull his wiry hands away from each other. "There's nothing there." My touch seems to distract him, because now he's playing with my fingers like a little kid, bending them together and pulling them into shapes.

"Oh, shit!" Lucifer squeaks, his eyes now focused directly upwards, and he struggles against the seat belt as it digs into his neck. "Fucking crocodiles."

I can't really say I know what's going on in his head now, but he's watching the car ceiling like it's a particularly thrilling movie.

He shifts again, slouching down in his seat, lifting his knees, and planting them in the back of Dagen's seat.

"Lucifer, get your fucking knees out of my back," Dagen growls.

"I don't think he really knows what he's doing right now," I try to explain, but Dagen looks so pissed that I attempt to get Luce's feet back on the floor.

Lucifer is giggling and clapping and all in all sounding like a fucking one-man marching band, his ceiling movie having apparently ended. His noises are indescribable, part barnyard, part Neanderthal, part machine. This time, I can't shut him up; he won't let me any nearer to him, his limbs flailing wildly in imitation of a perturbed flamingo.

"*For fuck's sakes, shut him up!*" Dag yells. His patience having given up completely, he turns to face us, a glare on his face.

"*Watch the fucking road!*" I scream back, and Dagen turns, grabbing the wheel and swerving sharply because we had halfway drifted into another fucking lane. I sink back into my seat, trying to ignore Luce's ravings and Dagen's fuming. Dag's even madder now. His yelling hasn't accomplished anything but to make him look stupid. We do, however, manage to get back to my apartment in one piece.

I put on *Baraka* in hopes of entertaining Lucifer when we get in. Dagen stomps to my room and slams the door. Fucking sixth-grader, I swear. I force another bottle of water into Luce's hands, cap already screwed off.

"Drink," I order.

He manages to down about half the bottle before the TV successfully captures all of his attention and he sinks into it, talking at length to whichever faces appear onscreen. I figure he's dealt with temporarily. Guess I'll attend to the other patient.

I open my door timidly, which is stupid, because it's my door and I should be able to open it however the fuck I want, because I shouldn't have some hyper-druggie in my living room or a fucking drama queen in my bedroom, and yet I have both. Go fucking figure.

Dagen is standing moodily by my window, his arms crossed, his glare bordering on deadly. His too-black hair with his too-long bangs in combination with his sloping posture and his unrecognized pout is frankly enough to make me grin. Which is not exactly the reaction Dagen was hoping for, I don't think.

"What?" he hisses at me.

I shrug to keep myself from laughing.

"*What?*"

I'm almost laughing now. "You just look so...fucking emo." Obviously the wrong thing to say, but I knew that. I'd say that Dagen's expression has altered from a glare to a glower.

"*And I have fucking good reason. He could've fucking died, Benjamin!*"

I'm not smiling now.

"I know, Dag," I say, and I sit on the bed facing him. He looks drained. Finally, he crosses over from the window to sit next to me.

I don't have to say anything more.

Dagen falls tiredly back onto the bed. He prods at my arm, and I get what he wants, so I lie back, too. I listen to him sigh.

"You alright?" I ask, and I know he knows that I don't mean about Doug. I just mean about him.

"Yeah," he says, finally.

We're lying across my bed widthwise; the corner of my eye can see the steady rise/fall of his chest. In the background, we can hear Lucifer muttering excitedly to the television screen.

"He's fucked," Dagen comments.

"Utterly." I sigh. "Guess I should go check on him."

Dagen stands. "Let me."

I look at the clock. Just after seven in the morning. I think this could qualify as my most emotionally tumultuous night ever, what with Doug and...

I lick my lips. With all the hospital stuff, I'd almost forgotten about what may or may not have happened earlier.

Dagen re-enters my room. "He's fine. Well, he's high, but seems to be enjoying himself."

"That stuff lasts a long time, I think."

"We'll keep an eye on him."

He sprawls across the bed again, this time from the other side, I haven't moved, so his head is about at my shins.

Our hands are touching vaguely. I thought it was coincidental. But now...

Dagen's linking his fingers with mine, skimming pads across my open palm and fingers. His actions are again semi-absent, like he's filling in time or distracting himself. But it's intimate. This isn't something you do unless...

I know I should stop him because I'm just going to let myself get hurt, or whatever.

But I don't. I can't. It's just so fucking nice.

He's detailing my wrist now, tapping fingertips to veins and tracing bones. It hits me that I want this, and I don't mean just him doing this to me. I want this with him, this closeness. But I don't think I can stand, for even a second longer, to have this unacknowledged. I can't breathe, or I don't think I can.

But if I can't breathe, how is it that I'm preparing to speak? It's hard. This could end everything, yet I'm trying to convince myself that I'm better than some fucking toy and I need to kick the whole take-what-I-can-get syndrome, and I won't let him just...

"Dag." Wow. A whole syllable, I'm impressed. "What are we—"

"Why don't you want me?" he interrupts me. His voice is calm, curious, as if it's something he really doesn't understand.

I can't find my voice. It's lost somewhere. I... What? "What?" I choke on the word.

"Why don't you want me?" he says again, his voice just as conversational and sure. "Everybody else wants me, but never you."

"Dag..." I can't say it. Saying it will be suicide. If I say it, I'm handing it all over to him. And I'll lose. I know it. So I won't say it.

"I do." Fuck.

I said it.

He's suddenly over me, face upside down, just inches above me, and he kisses me then, forcefully, lips giving way almost immediately to tongue, and I'm pinned to the bed without him even touching me anywhere else, hands supporting him next to my head, this topsy-turvy angle. I'm absolutely immobilized, except I know I'm moving, reacting, pulsing my tongue against his as he enters my mouth, eyes pinched shut because I'm refusing to acknowledge but I want so badly to acknowledge, because it feels fucking amazing, and this is just lips and tongue and mouth.

I finally dart my face away and to the side, wiping my mouth with the back of my hand. Staring heatedly into his upside-down eyes because I *can't*, I can't be that way with him, still half convinced it will never mean anything for him, just another entertaining conquest.

"What?" he asks, his breath shaky like his hand, first contact, fingers to my jawbone and palm to my temple, against my cheek, somehow coaxing me to meet his eyes, "Benji, what?"

"I can't." I try to look away, but I'm sunk. His fucking blue eyes like quicksand won't let me leave.

"You already have." He tries to kiss me again, and I want to move away, I do, but his lips find mine anyway, gentler this time, persistent as they establish contact.

"Stop it," I whisper.

"Benji…" he murmurs.

"Stop it!"

He pulls away, and I sit up awkwardly, sliding backwards to lean against a bedpost, knees bent, held to my chest: a barrier. He sits cross-legged beside me, facing my side. "Why?" he asks, and he doesn't touch me.

"How many people have you slept with, Dagen?" I'm not looking at him.

"I told you already."

"And how many names do you remember? How many of them did you make feel like this? Good and important and wanted."

He doesn't answer. He knows I know.

"And I can't just be one forty-nine, Dagen. I can't be your latest win, just another unhappy victim of Dagen Mercutio who thought for one perfect second that they actually stood a fucking chance."

He looks at me. I can almost see the hazel of my eyes reflected in the blue of his. There is silence.

"Brown," he whispers, finally.

"What?" Because I think for a stupid second he's talking about my eyes.

"Brown," he repeats. "Dagen Mercutio Brown. You know me, Benjamin, Benji, you are the only one who knows me, the only one..."

"Stop saying that! Everyone is always the only one! You make everyone feel like they are the single most important living creature in the world, and all you have to do is look into their stupid eyes and they believe every fucking word you say, even if they know, and I *know*, that it's a lie. I don't know you, Dagen, no one does. You just make them feel like they do."

"Maybe I do," he says slowly, "Maybe I make the whole world feel like they are the only one. I don't know, Ben, I don't work at it. But...you. You are the one that makes me feel that."

"That's not true," I whisper, cracking.

"Yes, it is."

"Don't you get it, Dag?"

He kneels and bends in towards me, his hand bracketing my head and his lips near mine, again, dragging over my jawline, cornering my mouth.

"Get what?" he breathes.

"I'm in love with you." I laugh derisively. "You know I am. And you'll only end up trashing my heart."

"I won't."

"How do you know?"

"Because if I did, I'd fucking break my own, okay?"

I laugh. This is the most bizarre conversation I've ever heard in my whole life. I tell him so. He grins.

"We'll put it in a song. Heart trashing on the I90."

I roll my eyes, and drop my knees a bit. I let him kiss my throat, my eyes closed, just feeling. And it feels fucking amazing. His hand guides my face so our lips meet and we kiss again, and I let myself do it fully.

"So?" he asks, after a few minutes.

"So, what?"

"So…can we? Try, like…being together?" This level of uncertainty on Dagen is disconcerting.

"We're always together." I try to lighten things up, but he doesn't let me.

"You know what I mean."

"Yeah, I know. Yeah. Alright. Just. Give me a bit to get my head around it."

"Why? You not sure about me?"

"I'm more than sure—I don't trust you to not realize I'm me and leave."

He cocks an eyebrow at me. "That so? I'm going to have to prove myself?"

"Mmm-hmm," I agree.

He laughs, softly. He tugs a little at my ear with his mouth, but then, like maybe he can't help himself, he tilts my face and kisses me head-on. This time, I kiss him back.

"I've wanted this, Benj, more than you…get." I barely catch it. But my insides are playing a fucking symphony in my honour as our lips connect again and again.

***

Dagen has manoeuvred me so I'm lying lengthwise on the bed. His one hand takes hold of my hair and the other palms my chest over my t-shirt. I've never been kissed like this before. His tongue explores all the areas of my mouth with determination, like if he doesn't do it now he might not get another chance. His lips are sure and strong and in control. I wonder vaguely if this should bother me, if I should be fighting this, stop being passive or something. I play at taking control for a little bit, but I guess it's just nice to let him direct, because it's good. He kisses even better than I figured he would.

His mouth leaves mine, and my eyes open as he shifts his efforts to my neck, swirling the tip of his tongue around the "O" his lips form at different spots on my throat. The movements are achieving what I'm guessing is the desired effect, because my dick hardens. I feel stupidly embarrassed because I know he can feel it, and some juvenile little voice in my head is all, "Ben, you know this is a dude you're making out with, right?"

But that feeling doesn't last, because he's at my lips again, moaning lowly before shifting to my ear, his pelvis tilted against mine and making it pretty clear that I'm not the only one turned on here. He adds pressure, generating friction, and I'm responding pretty damn completely. I let myself grip his ribs, his ass, pressing him into me. All I want is for him and me to ditch our goddamn cock-blocking clothes and rub one out together, just like this. But once again, my ever-inconvenient sense of responsibility kicks in and, with great mental effort, I shove him off.

"Hungh!!" he grunts in surprise and annoyance. "What the fuck, man?"

"Luce," I say, gingerly rearranging my still-hard dick and straightening my shirt.

"Oh, fucking Christ. He's fine."

"He's fucking high and alone, Dag. We can't just leave him there, and you fucking know it."

"Can we leave him there for just a little while longer?" Dagen tries, sliding his compact body up against mine. He tongues my ear and palms my cock, and I'm so, so fucking tempted. "Jesus, Benji," he whispers. "You just feel so fucking good."

I want it. I want to stay here and be touched and see his smug, angled face as he gets off above me, but now that I've thought about Luce and everything that could go wrong, I probably wouldn't be able to come, anyway.

"Come on, man," I urge. "You want the first time we fuck for me to be thinking about Luce the whole time? Because I'd rather not." I force myself to push Dagen's hand away. "That and I don't want him to wreck my shit."

"Christ," Dagen whines, standing when I stand. "If that little fucker ever touches this shit again, I'm going to mash his face in."

"Well, your intentions aren't honourable, but I guess the end result will be the same," I quip.

Dagen follows me grumpily into the living room where Luce has entered full alien mode. I sit on the couch to monitor him. Dagen joins me. He sits too close, his hand at my thigh, and his teeth at my shoulder until Luce falls asleep spread-eagle on the floor, and we do, too, cramped and frustrated on the sofa.

Chapter Nine

Two days later, Dagen arrives with uncharacteristic promptness to pick me up for our first official date. Which I think is officially ridiculous, because we hang out *all the fucking time*. He says it's something he's always wanted to do. He's never really...dated. And I think that's weird for me.

He buzzes up and knocks instead of just walking in.

He even brought flowers.

"I actually kind of hate you," I tell him when he shoves them at me.

"Put them in water."

"In what, Dag? You think I'm swimming in vases over here?"

He looks momentarily disappointed, but starts digging through my cupboards before finally surfacing with a wide-mouth Nalgene. Then he roots through the drawers until he's brandishing a pair of scissors.

"You're supposed to cut the stems diagonally under running water," he informs me and does it himself. I give him a blank look. "I told my mom I was going on a date. And she said to take flowers. And I said, 'Mom, I have no fucking clue what to do with flowers.' So she showed me. Don't look at me like that."

"Can we just go and get this over with?" I ask.

"Glad to see you, too," he responds with a decent amount of snark. Finally, he seems satisfied with the bouquet and turns around to face me, and suddenly we're standing in my doorway and I realize: I can kiss him. Like, he would even like it if I kissed him. Like, he is maybe even hoping or expecting that I will. So I do, eyes open and curious. His lips are hard, ungenerous, and I find myself touching him—my palm along his jaw, fingers on his cheek—just for a second.

"Tell me again how much you hate me," he murmurs when I pull away.

I shrug and maybe even blush a little. He kisses the corner of my mouth, smiles oddly, and leads me towards the door with a light touch on the small of my back.

**

"Still haven't got a hybrid," I note, as we climb into his car.

"Not since yesterday," he replies, unapologetic.

"Do you like fish?"

"Is that a...trick question?"

"No. It means that you're really going to blame yourself when the fucking oceans dry up and all the fish are dead."

He laughs. "And you say I'm dramatic."

"It's a real fucking thing! Like, we're such a throwaway culture and—"

"Okay, Enviro-Boy, I hear ya. But it would be kind of *more* wasteful to go out and buy a brand-new car when I've already got one that works fine."

"I guess," I admit.

"You know I'm right. But next time I buy a car, I will try to consider the environment if it'll save me the fucking lecture."

I make a noncommittal noise, and he grabs my thigh and squeezes, sways it back and forth for a second. "Now, will you cheer the fuck up, sweetness? This was supposed to just be a fun thing."

"Yeah. Sorry." I like the solidity of his hand on me.

"How's Doug?" he asks. "Heard anything since yesterday?"

"Yeah, he's fine. I called Abby this morning, and she said they sent him home yesterday. Just needs to take it easy. Consider, you know, not taking mystery drugs, drink water. Shit like that. She said he was snoring on the couch as we spoke, so that is kind of a relief."

"That's good."

"Yeah," I agree.

"And Luce?"

"Feeling pretty shitty. Feels bad about everything."

"Yeah, well, he fucking well should," Dagen says darkly.

"It wouldn't kill you to cut him some slack, you know."

"Wouldn't kill him to not be a stupid shit sack."

I snort. "You knew what you were getting into with him from day one. He's not exactly an enigma."

"Yeah, and for the music, that's great. I just don't want him around the rest of the time."

I shrug. "Guess he only bothers me when I'm hungover."

"Because you're a goddamn saint, Benji." He reaches over to, like, what, ruffle my hair? I smack his hand away and tell him to watch the road. He takes that to mean slide his hand over my leg again. He slowly slips it between my thighs, until I shift nervously, and then returns it to the wheel. My neck warms and my diaphragm wrings itself out. I look out the window.

"Feels good, doesn't it?"

"What?" I ask, not sure if we're referring to the conversation or something else.

"I dunno," he replies. "This. Us."

"Fuck, I don't know, Dag. It feels like it always feels. Good. Normal. Fuck," I lie. Because it feels more than good. It feels significant and like coming home, and I'm so wound up I think I might pass out and I'm terrified of it.

"Why, Benjamin," he replies, his voice high and breathy with mock surprise, "it's almost as though you don't want to talk about your feelings."

"Jesus, you're an asshole."

He laughs like he's just the wittiest thing, then slips his palm alongside mine, interlaces our fingers, and drops both our hands in his lap.

And maybe it feels big and scary, but also it does feel good. Normal. Weird. Weird-normal. Good. It feels really fucking good.

***

He takes me to the motherfucking Sky restaurant thing at the top of the Needle.

I'm so not even sort of amused as he push-pulls me towards the elevator. "Jesus fuck, Dag. No. I am not fucking going up there. Jesus, how lame can you get? Seriously, can we please just go somewhere chill?"

"Come on!" he counters, all smiles and cheer. "I'll bet you haven't been here in years."

"I've never been here," I correct him. "My parents always assured me that it was a lame-ass tourist thing with not-that-great food."

"Who gives a fuck about the food, Ben, when you've got such gracious company? Not to mention that, due to my massive celebrity, I got to knock some poor schmuck off the reservation list, and goddamn if that didn't feel good."

"Oh, Christ. You called and demanded a table? Seriously? What is *wrong* with you?"

"Oh, relax, I didn't *demand* anything. I just casually hinted that it would be truly appreciated should a table be made available."

"And how did you know no one's called the fucking press?" I can't help but hiss.

"Calm yourself, my dear," Dagen replies archly, and I feel my eyes roll upward, heaven fucking help me. "This isn't *that* sort of an establishment."

"You're the literal worst," I concede.

"I still can't believe you've lived here your whole life and never actually been here."

"You know my parents." I shrug. "If it's not legit ethnic or wholly local, it's not worth the bother." The elevator doors open at the top. "Well, let's go give in to the Man, then."

"Sugar, you're a pop icon. You're the Man's wet dream," Dagen murmurs under his breath, then smiles stunningly at the hostess.

"Hot tip," I offer once we're seated. "You probably shouldn't refer to your date as, you know, a mass of corporate jizz if you're planning on scoring."

Jesus. I force myself not to blush. Because he'll be fucking scoring with me, and I somehow keep forgetting that and then re-remembering, and it makes me this weird combination of hideously nervous and desperately horny.

Dagen just smirks, "Oh? I'll keep that in mind."

***

He's kind of stupidly adorable. A bottle of wine helps take the edge of my curmudgeonly skepticism, and the changing view of the city really is pretty.

But he fucking pays, which, admittedly, he has done a thousand other times for Slurpees or lunches or Go-Karts or whatever, and I've never even thought about it, just said, "Oh, hey, thanks, man, I'll get you next time." And I do, and that's it. But this is like a date-thing, and I don't know if it *means* something, and if it does, what exactly that meaning might be.

"What was that?" I demand on the drive home.

"What was what?" he asks distractedly, checking his mirror. He's probably bummed because no one asked for his autograph. Guess he doesn't realize he's going to have to hit trendier spots— or younger—think school grounds younger—if he wants his ego stroked.

"The you-paying-for-my-food thing."

"I told you, I was taking you out on a date," he replies mildly.

"Well, I can pay for myself."

He snorts. "We get the same checks. I know you can pay for yourself. I just wanted to pay for you tonight. Like you used to pay for Lillian."

"Yeah, well she expected it. I don't."

"I know." He grins, remembering. "You had to get that shit job at Denny's just to finance her. High fucking maintenance."

"Don't have to remind me. But still. I can pay for myself. I don't like having people pay for me."

"I like paying," he insists.

"Cool story, bro," I bark back. "I don't like you paying."

"Jesus Christ, are you making this a thing?"

"I'm not fucking making it a thing. It *is* a thing."

"It's not a fucking thing, Benj, Jesus."

"It is a fucking thing!" I know the easy thing would be to drop it, but I just can't. "I'm still getting my head around this whole you-and-me deal as it is. I can't handle weird power shit like this, too, okay?

Dagen half smiles and knocks his knuckles against my knee. "Alright. I hear you. It's officially not a thing? I just wanted to do this right. And doing it right doesn't mean freaking you out, so... you can spot me next time, cool?"

"Yeah." I exhale. "Yeah, alright."

***

"Are you inviting me up?" he asks as he pulls into a guest spot at my building.

"Jesus, would you stop making this weird?"

"Making what weird?"

"I don't want to date," I say, frustrated.

"What?" he asks, sort of freezing.

"Shit. Not like that. I mean—stop making it weird. You said it's just like us, so can we please just be us? You know after a night out you're gonna come up and crash at my place, so can we

86

just cut to that? Except maybe with like, I dunno, hand jobs or something?"

Dagen cackles, throwing his head back luxuriously. I see the outline of his Adam's apple in the dark, along with a few random neck hairs his razor didn't catch. His hands tighten on the wheel and his eyelids crinkle closed, and I want him entirely to myself.

So, when he flings open the car door and unfolds himself to stand, I notice it immediately.

"You weren't wearing your seat belt," I accuse him.

He gives me a curious look. "Sorry, Officer, my mistake?"

"Jesus, Dagen, if I'm going to get fucking emotionally involved with you, I'm not super interested in worrying about you losing your remaining brain cells in some stupid accident." I sound borderline hysterical and I know it.

"I'm not exactly Safety Boy," he replies, head cocked, eyes careful. "And I'm pretty sure you've been emotionally involved with me for the majority of our lives..."

"Not, like, officially," I say, and I can practically taste how lame it sounds.

Dagen snorts and shakes his head. "Now who's making it fucking weird? C'mon, sweetness, let's just go upstairs, alright? You're wound up so tight I think you're gonna give yourself an aneurysm. Besides, I think somebody mentioned hand jobs?"

***

Once inside, I toss my keys on the counter. "What do you wanna do?"

Dagen grins. "What do you fucking think?" He takes one, two steps and he's in my space. There's a suspended moment. The corner of his mouth twitches upwards, dimpling his cheek. He slides a warm, steady hand up my neck, fingers contouring in around the back of my ear.

"I've been fucking wanting you all night. Even if you are acting sorta intense," he informs me, before his lips crash into mine. I copy his movements, feel his skin and stubble under my careful fingertips. He steps in impossibly closer. He makes a needy little noise and presses our foreheads together before sinking his teeth into my lip. I barely have time to whine before he follows over the tender spot with stripes of his tongue. And we're making out. Like...well, like we do whenever we're on the road. Just this time...with each other. And we're not drunk. And we're not... this isn't a one-time thing.

I give him a querying look. He shrugs. "I like gauging your reactions."

"You're creepy, you know that?"

"Creepy, or considerate?" he challenges before pressing his lips back against mine, his hands cold but welcome on the skin under my shirt. He sucks thoughtfully on my lower lip, and I'm pressing close, a concentrated thrill of arousal striking through me, tangible as a pickaxe.

"Arms," he demands.

I free my limbs and let him strip off my shirt. He runs his hands hungrily over my chest. I watch his eyes as he touches me. He backs me onto the couch and straddles me: graceful, natural, easy, his mouth fastened onto my neck until he breaks off just to look. His hands are slow, somehow, devouring every bit of me, and I swear I have never been wanted quite like this.

"Goddammit, Benji, I—fuck." He breathes, and he's invading my mouth again, almost too brutally, with too much need. His teeth trap my lip, and he nips at it again. It hurts. It's not teasing, it is just straight up painful, but I find myself groaning, gripping his t-shirt in my fists and pressing up into him. I can't shake the feeling of reassurance that comes with his confidence in this. All I want is to soak up the evidence of his need.

I kiss his jaw carefully, and he bucks into me, cock hard against my thigh. It sends a spike of something through me. I grind against it.

"Jesus, Dag…" I whisper, and it is like my words open some kind of floodgate because suddenly he's murmuring steadily against my skin.

"Fuck, sweetness, the things I want to do with you. To you. Sometimes it is all I can do to keep myself from dropping to my knees every fucking time I see you just so I can take your load down my throat. Every cock I have sucked I've imagined is yours, do you know that? Imagining I have been practising for you, so I could fucking rock your world if you ever gave me the chance. Please Benj, let me suck you. I wanna taste you. I'll make it good, I swear to God, I'll make it so fucking good…"

The filthy words coming out of his perfect mouth are too much, and I am rabbiting my hips up, clothed cock sliding alongside his.

"Jesus, Dag you gotta stop or I'll—"

"You gonna come, sugar?" he demands, eagerly, and his hands are scrabbling at my fly, wasting no time reaching into my boxers and gripping my cock, firmly, unquestioningly. "Do it, please, Benj, I want you to. Do you have any idea how long I have been wanting this? Fucking desperate to watch you, feel it on me, taste you…"

I can't quite bite back the cry that pours from my mouth as I peak, shuddering, spurting out messily across his shirt.

"Fuck," Dag mutters. "Fuck, stay. Just like that. Just for a minute." He quickly bares his own cock, jeans slipping low. He swipes a nearly shaking hand through the jizz pooling on my stomach and flashes me a filthy grin. His hand tightens around his cock, and he jerks himself, smooth and quick, as I stay snared below him, eyes not big enough to see all I want to see. The hand not on his cock comes up to touch my face. His fingers press into my cheek while his thumb traces my bottom lip. My spent cock twitches at the intensity of it all.

"You watching?" he asks, voice still low and seductive. I nod, feeling shaky with spent adrenaline. I am fixated on the movement of his pale hand along his reddening cock.

"Good." He sighs. "I love your eyes on me. I feel them, you know. When you're trying not to. Love the way your eyes follow me around a room, makes me hard. Makes me imagine you between my legs, begging for it. God, I wanna make you beg, Benji. Make you squirm and whine and plead until I shoot off all over your pretty, perfect face. Shit. Fuck. Kiss me, fuck, fuck, gorgeous, need you!"

I am half stunned at the decadent obscenities spewing from his mouth and don't really even have time to react before he's slamming his mouth against mine, emitting a guttural groan and coming hard, erupting over his hand, heating my skin. I find my head riveted between both of his hands as he kisses me deeply for a long moment before finally pulling away, his forehead against mine. "Fuck. God. Fuck, Benj, so good."

"Yeah," is all my mush-brain can come up with, but I'm smiling and he doesn't stop kissing me.

"You're something else, you know that?"

And the words are like ice water running a slick course down my spine. I pull back jerkily. His smile freezes.

"What?" he asks with urgency and concern.

I awkwardly unseat him. Fasten my pants. Heart pounding in my ears, face flushing. Because I have heard those words before. By him. But not to me.

I skitter towards the kitchen and wash my hands, unable to face him.

"Babe, what?" he repeats.

I whirl on him. He's got his shirt off and is using it to wipe himself. He drops in on the counter and looks at me, waiting. My hands tense up. Like every fear I have has just been confirmed and it has been what, three days?

"Jesus Christ," I spit. "Don't."

"Don't what?" His eyes are big under a furrowed brow.

"Use those, like, generic lines on me. Don't fucking call me babe when I have heard you call everyone that to the point of it not evening meaning anything. It weirds me out and I don't like it."

He just looks at me blankly. "I…" he starts, then stops. Licks his bottom lip, drags it into his mouth, then releases. He tentatively extends a hand to touch my forearm. Part of me wants to jerk away but the rest of me just wants him. "Okay…and you couldn't have just said that? Like. Did you need to go storming off on me?"

"Jesus, Dagen. Don't you get that this is literally exactly what I am afraid of? Just being another fucking Jon or Cori?"

"Who?" He stares at me.

"Oh my god, seriously? Why do I remember the names of the people you've fucked and you don't?!" I'm not even mad anymore, it is just fucking bizarre.

"I don't remember them because they don't matter! They are not a thing. You are. You matter. It's just fucking sex with them. They know it, I know you. And that's not what I'm in for with you. I have been pretty fucking clear about that. But, like, I won't call you babe if you don't want me to, no problem."

"It's not just that. I just need you to…not use lines."

"Okay…" He stretches the vowel dubiously. "And how do I know what is a line and what's not?"

"If you've said it to someone else, it's a line!" I flounder.

"You're being kind of ridiculous, you know that, right? I've said a lot of shit to a lot of people. And what about stuff I have said that you haven't overheard? What category does that fall into?" His thoughts are falling fast and frustrated. "And you know I would kind of rather be thinking about being with you when I am with you, not my fucking word selection."

I scrub the base of my palm over my forehead, stumbling a bit. "I just—I want stuff between us to be specific to us. I don't want to be second guessing if we're in this or not." I bite my lip, pleading silently for him to just get it. "I need you to be genuine," I mumble, beyond pathetic.

Dagen sighs and tosses his head. "Can you give me a fucking break, Benjamin? I was just trying to make it good for you. Make sure you got off and didn't freak out. It was fucking good. I've wanted you for basically ever and it felt fantastic to finally have you, and all I fucking wanted was to convey that to you, alright? That's it. I wasn't trying to use any lines or whatever." His eyes are hot angry embers. "Jesus, you know I don't know what the hell I'm doing. I've never had a fucking girlfriend before, let alone a wife," he says bitingly, "so sorry if I'm not a fucking relationship guru!"

And with that, he bolts towards the door, yanking his hoodie off the hook. The motion is not smooth enough, and the hood catches. He pulls harder, but in the same direction, and I hear the seams protest warningly.

"Where are you going?" I can't quite keep the surprise out of my voice, because I've never seen Dagen give up on anything, not ever.

"Getting the fuck out of here. This was a shit idea, anyhow." He struggles stupidly with the hoodie, one arm in and the other flailing as it seeks, and fails to find, the other hole. His voice is low with angry defeat, and it almost physically hurts. I'm not used to this kind of Dagen.

"Wait, Dag, don't." I stand between him and the door, one palm out, defensive.

"Move."

"Dag. Please." I repeat, feeling stupid. I'm shirtless, trying to convince my best friend-turned-boyfriend not to run away from my apartment after the most sexually charged, and, frankly, gratifying experience of my life.

"What?" His tone hitches with rage or…

Oh.

Upset.

I can deal with Dagen upset. I've done it a million times.

"Hey," I say, allowing myself a small, soothing half-smile. "Don't be a moron."

"I'm not being a fucking moron," he grumbles, but I know he's realizing he's on familiar ground here.

"Yeah," I counter, affectionately, "you are. Come on. Sit. We'll talk. We'll figure it out. I promise."

This is my magic string of words. I use it sparingly, but when I do, it works. I used it to get Dagen to sign on with our label, KXV, which he didn't think was flashy enough, which he didn't think was offering us a good enough royalty rate, but which was stable and kept the money flowing in. I used it to get him to be my best man. I used it one night when Miranda went briefly missing and Dagen came as close as I've ever seen him to legit melting down.

"Fine," he spits, collapsing onto a barstool, refusing to look at me. His bangs fall over his eyes and he shakes them off, his black hoodie finally on, but unzipped over his bare chest. His cum-smeared t-shirt is still clasped in his fist. I stand before him, leaning against the speckled, granite breakfast bar.

"I'm sorry." I say quietly. "I am just kinda twitchy is all."

"Whatever," he responds cattily, swivelling away from me.

"Dag…" I step in behind him, tentatively touch his shoulder. "I just freaked."

He sighs again, letting himself lean back and into me a little bit. I slide my hands down his chest and cross my arms just below his neck. I kiss his ear.

"I'm sorry," I repeat. "You weren't trying to make me feel shitty, and I should have known that."

He is still tense against me. A suspended silence grows then ebbs, and I feel him give.

"Fine," he agrees, slightly less sulkily. Which, with Dag, is sometimes the best you can hope to get.

I kiss his temple, and we stay like that for a long moment.

Finally, I grab us a couple of beers and slide onto the barstool next to him, our shoulders knocking comfortably.

"I still don't know how this works, Ben," he says after a while.

"Can't help you there," I reply, uselessly. "But we'll figure it out. Let's just chill for a bit, though, okay? Put on a DVD or something." He dumbly walks towards my shelves. I put my beer on a coaster and sink back into the couch cushions. I can't quite make out what he selects, but he fiddles with the player and comes to join me until we are sitting close, like we always do, but not touching.

"Fuck this," I hear Dagen say under his breath. "Shove." He pushes me forward, worming his way behind me, until he is occupying the full length of the couch. He's not graceful or subtle at all.

"Lie down," he demands.

I'm awkward about it, too. It still feels too new and foreign.

Dagen snorts and grabs me, yanking me close until he's curled around my back, palm against my skin just above my hip.

Within a few breaths, I relax, acclimatize to the contact, and find I'm more than alright with it.

Chapter Ten

WE DON'T HAVE a ton of time to recoup after getting home from tour before the less musical part of the job rears its head again. When I'm home, and it's just me hanging out with Dagen or Lillian or visiting my parents or whatever, it's weird, but I almost forget. I'm not that recognizable without eyeliner, apparently, and Seattle doesn't exactly have a lot of star seekers. Nevertheless, it's eight days before Christmas, and we're getting made-up for a gig at MTV. Dagen's stoked. He's no good at down time. It's not that we haven't been doing anything. We've mostly finished off two new songs already, and we're booked to head into the studio in April, with a tentative release date for late August—which means another tour starting September.

Until then, we've got to keep the hype going: music and teen rags; the occasional unplugged gig. Matty, our agent, is not so subtly pushing for a full-out relocation to L.A. for the parties and networking. He knows the business, and I know I should consider it, but the hassle hardly seems worth it when it's just a quick flight away. I try to appease him by following orders, accepting that I don't know shit about the industry, really. Dagen's less relaxed. He's got ideas, suggestions, a whole fucking vision. Probably pisses Matty off, but I stay out of it. Dagen usually pisses everyone off after a while.

Dag and I have slid scarily easily into our relationship thing. I guess it's not like much has changed. Gaming, jamming, and drinking with the added bonus of getting off. Somehow, we haven't really gotten around to telling anyone. Dagen continues to torment me in public, never quite doing enough for anyone to suspect anything, and why would they?

Our purpose, so far as Matty is concerned, is as angsty eye candy with an ounce of creativity and passable talent. Our job is to be appealing to white, semi-affluent teenage girls who have cash to spend on CDs and, more importantly, merch.

We're the product they're buying, and what they are buying is straight guys who could, just maybe, fall for them. Dag swoons melodramatically when I talk like this, and calls me his darling cynic, but it's not like he can deny it. I'm not mad about it, but I'm not gonna pretend like this whole deal isn't about making rich men richer. And it's not like we don't get paid.

What I'm still not used to is makeup. Pale-ish foundation, I hate how it feels, thick and suffocating as the un-made-up makeup artist slathers it on. It provides a base for the careful lines of liquid eyeliner that spiral from my left caruncula to pattern delicately outwards across my cheek. I look like an artfully sad clown. I swear I didn't know I was getting into this. What happened to garage bands?

Dagen's got a red-and-black diamond painted on, slicing his eye just like Scar from *The Lion King*. He catches me looking at him and purses his lips to form the gentlest of air kisses—careful not to smear his flawless lipstick. I feel the corners of my mouth flick upwards.

Since it is a more intimate venue, the costuming is less extreme. Jeans and band t-shirts that cling a bit too tightly with V-necks that dip a bit too low. Doug's chest hair spurts out the top of his like water from a whale's blow hole, and they quickly change him out of that and into a long-sleeved, buttoned-up flowered shirt that looks vaguely like a blouse. I guess it is supposed to be ironic. It seems muted under the mountain-man rusty-red beard Doug has been growing. Doug doesn't seem fussed.

Dagen is diagonally zipped into a tight, white hoodie while leather cuffs are snapped around my wrists. Luce gets green-and-black plaid pants with suspenders that flop uselessly beside his hips. His t-shirt has some red-and-black version of *The Scream* splattered on it. Despite my cynicism, the excitement gets to me.

The glue on my not-quite-obviously fake eyelashes itches as it dries. The hands of the makeup team fly, double-checking eyeliner and perfecting imperfections that only they can see.

This is it, then. Live studio audience. People who have paid literal money to see us. The least we can do is look the part. We're ushered out of wardrobe and towards the main area. I hear the chattering calm and the whooping begin as one corner of the crowd catches sight of Dagen strutting in the lead. The thrill courses through the crowd. The lights are hot and my blood is zinging, and maybe it's not *just* about rich men getting richer after all.

***

After our set, there is a short break. Our costume makeup is scoured from our faces in favour of the standard. It doesn't feel any less greasy or cover any less of our faces, but it is a lot less decorative: unnaturally natural with extra eyeliner. The dark lashes stay in place, too.

"Not that you need them," my makeup artist assures me.

Sweaty shirts are stripped off us—a dresser I didn't even know was there mops hastily at my pits, neck, and back—and replaced with not-sweaty shirts: black, black, and black, with a maroon one for Dagen. He is right where he thrives, and he looks fucking good. I want to touch him, to roast in his radiance.

His eyes find mine across the overstuffed room, and his smile is slow and deep and sumptuous. It satiates me, for now.

Soon enough, we're perched on tall wooden stools around Noelle, our VJ. Her gold hair is in a high pony on the back of her head. She's got big silver hoops which sway pleasantly from her earlobes. She wears a bodysuit-tight pink tank top with short jean shorts over black tights with slouchy little boots.

I think about fucking her. I think she'd be enthusiastic, like she is now, and she'd focus on my ego. Telling me how good I felt, how good I made her feel. Like everything I did brought her to the brink. She'd writhe prettily beneath me, and her tits would fit just right in my hands. She'd come easy and often. I wonder idly if she would fuck me, if I made it known I was interested.

This whole array of thoughts surprises me. Am I interested? Could I go for her if I was? Or does being with Dagen mean no more women, and does that bother me? I feel stupid, almost blindsided, for not figuring this shit out already, but I have no chance to unpack it now. The friendly chat is coming on fast.

We're going through the expected stuff. Explaining that no, Doug didn't overdose; it was a simple allergic reaction. Shellfish. As if Doug eats anything that isn't cheeseburgers. Kell, our publicist, had us rehearse this lie prior to the interview, and it flows smooth and genuine out of Dagen's mouth.

"The current record has a more playful, almost flirtatious edge to it," Dagen is BS-ing, "like the second-date album, you know?" Noelle nods, her expression serious, absorbent. "We were really bolstered by the energy our fans brought to the table, but we were also inquisitive, pushing at boundaries, pulling ourselves open to see what makes us tick.

"Our newer stuff, the stuff that will likely appear on our next album come summer, is more personal. It also has a duality to it: the knowing and the not knowing, the comfort and the strangeness."

Jesus, Dagen is laying the creative shit on thick. Not that I try to interject. Dag's the one everyone wants to hear from, anyway, being lead singer and all. Kell has put Luce on a strict deferral policy, because he'll ramble, and it's embarrassing. Always direct the questions back to Dagen, Kell insists, and Luce, thankfully, obeys. Doug, of course, just doesn't talk. They don't even give him a microphone anymore.

"We're really excited by what's next," Dagen continues, sliding off a soft, easy question from Noelle. "The sound might be a bit different—more intimate—than our last couple because we were a bit uncertain with those two, not sure if we were just lucky or what. Now that we've got ourselves a kick-ass fan base—" that gets a loud, pleased reaction "—we're able to try some new things. Still us, but we're not so scared of losing our momentum," Dagen explains.

"Awesome!" Noelle grins, her teeth catching the light, almost shinier than her innumerable necklaces. "So, you guys head back to the studio come April, and I know we're all looking forward to what comes out! Anything else on the go for you?"

This one is low stakes, so Dag gives me a minute nod, indicating for me to take it.

"Well," I say, careful not to talk too loudly into the handheld mic, "we've gotta have something to actually take to the studio, so we'll just be working, mostly, writing and fiddling with whatever we come up with."

"Oh, but all work and no play..." Noelle teases.

I chuckle and attempt to be charismatic, knowing I am shitty at it. "Dag can be a bit of a hard ass."

"Still," she perseveres, "four gorgeous guys? You can't tell me you're *all* single!"

I feel my pits and palms prickle with sweat, and I try to will the blush away from my face. I dart my eyes at Dagen, desperate to find a way to *defer, defer, defer,* but he is just smirking at me, eyebrows high and mischievous. I clear my throat and switch the mic from my left hand to my right. Or try to. In reality, I drop the stupid fucking thing, drowning the studio audience in a painfully loud booming mess of sound.

Fuck shit goddamn mother of fucking Christ. The stupid thing is rolling around at my feet, and I fumble for it twice before managing to pick it up again. My face has flooded red past the abilities of even my professional-grade foundation, and Dagen is laughing his ass off. Half of me is terrified that his laughter is just a cover for the strip he will tear off me later for being a motherfucking amateur, but the audience has joined in with him cheerfully. I feel so fucking obvious I could choke. Instead, I sit quiet, eyes down, flushing and sweating miserably.

"Is that a yes?" Noelle giggles. I can't help but whip my eyes up to Dag's for reassurance. He gives me a charming little half-grin to let me know it's fine. It's just me dropping a mic, and it's no big deal. My heart is returning to normal speed and it's just fine, just fine, because he's got this. He was toying with me before, but he won't leave me unmoored.

"Have you *seen* Benjamin?" Dagen proclaims. "Who can resist such a dreamboat?"

The audience hoots out more laughter. The screen off to my left shows a cameraman zooming in on a "MAKE US YOUR SISTER WIVES, BENJAMIN" poster held up by a couple of flushed and thrilled girls, and I know it is a joke, but they are, like, fifteen, and it feels all kinds of fucked up.

"Not a soul," Noelle conspires. "So, are you gonna break hundreds of hearts tonight by telling us someone has stolen yours, Benjamin?" She presses the subject.

I flail, my tongue making useless noises as my fingers twist in my lap. My pulse rockets, sluicing the blood through my arteries in a way that is fast, too fast. Dagen snorts, and I feel the focus of the room shift to him as he raises the mic to his stupid, perfect mouth. I don't know what I'm more afraid of: Dagen saying something about him and me—or him denying it.

Logically, I know we cannot, *cannot* bring this up without discussing it with Kell first and developing some kind of a press strategy. Dagen has plenty of marketing savvy, and the intelligent part of my brain assures me of this. He is not a blurter. But warring with this logic is my useless, cautious heart, which is silently pleading with Dag to keep this small and contained and completely mine.

I'm holding my breath. Dagen brings the mic to his lips. His lips part. He's going to speak.

His gaze holds mine, like there aren't a hundred other people crowded around us and I trust him.

"Sorry to break it to you, folks," Dagen pronounces, "but our lovely Benjamin is totally taken."

Chapter Eleven

DESPITE NOELLE'S MANY pressing questions, Dagen refuses further comment, but apparently, according to Kell, at least, we've created tidal waves. But good ones? His words, not mine. Apparently, a secret relationship is exactly what one of us needs right now. I didn't tell him that it's what two of us have. With each other. Jesus, there is no way this whole thing ends in anything but destruction by fire. Apparently, I'm fine with that, though, because there's no way I'm moving to put an end to any of it.

Waiting to be alone with Dagen to interrogate him on *just what the hell was all that?* is torture, we're stripping and handing off clothing articles to smiling but slightly harried-looking staff while Kell natters cheerfully at us from Dag's cell which is on speaker and set upside down on a makeup cart. Eventually, we're dressed in our own clothing, the worst of the makeup has made it from our faces to remover wipes, and we are directed through a back door.

There're scores of teens in Allusion shirts, and we smile and sign CD jackets and posters and even a couple of arms; we hug fans and hold still long enough for the click and shutter of cameras before clambering into the car. Dagen throws a few kisses, his slight shoulders fitting through the open window. He hangs half out of it, waving as we pull away, until Doug manhandles him inside.

Dagen is glowing and kind of beautiful, sweaty hair, idiotic grin and everything. He loves this, truly, and knowing I had some small, skeptical part in getting him here heats my solar plexus in an odd, fluttery way. He claps Doug companionably on the shoulder then peers back over the leather seat at Luce and me.

"Okay back there?" he probes.

"Yeah, man," Luce replies and I nod.

"Good." Dagen beams. "Good. Awesome. That felt good. Went well. Thanks, guys."

Doug looks about as pleased as Doug ever looks, and Luce puffs up with the praise. I don't bother commenting that Dagen carried the show, as always, and the rest of us just followed his lead. We're tired and smug and high on popularity.

The feeling lasts until I'm alone in my hotel room. Kell wanted yet another phone conference, but Dagen said he would handle it solo. Luce can't sit still, and Doug never has anything to add. Dag knows I need some time away from people after spotlights and crowds. I put on my headphones and pull my iPod out of my bag, thumbing through my options. I decide to give Xiu Xiu another listen. I already have the CD at home.

Part of me knows I really should make the effort to switch to vinyl, but the pretension of it puts me off. I grew up on tapes and then CDs, so I guess I am a bit sentimental or something. Plus, vinyl covers are a bit unwieldy, and I have this ritual about new music. Listen to the album once, eyes closed, take it in. On the second listen, I follow along with the lyrics. Dagen tells me I go about it all wrong, that lyrics are secondary to the music, that I should focus on the feel, the mood, but I am too cerebral for all that. Plus, muttering artists piss me off. I want to know what they are saying, maybe it is important.

I'm a few tracks into my second listen—my laptop out so I can follow the lyrics online—when there is a knock on my door.

Ugh.

Except it's Dagen, so I can't say I'm actually all that upset. As far as people who are allowed around me when I want to be alone goes, Dagen is at the top of that list. Dagen might be the entirety of that list.

Once inside, he goes in to kiss me, and I meet his mouth easily. "Hey," I murmur into him, "what are you doing here?"

"Mmm," he answers against my lips. "Wanted to see you." He brackets me against the full-length mirror, arms on either side of my head, and kisses me enthusiastically, making appreciative noises in his throat. "That okay?" he asks, lips close to my ear as I rest my hands under the bottom of his hoodie against his skin. "What I said today?" he clarifies.

"Yeah," I reply, half surprised to find I'm being honest.

He slides back until his forehead is tilted against mine. He kisses my nose, and I give him a *seriously?* sort of look, which he deftly ignores.

"I know you don't love attention," he continues, "and Kell said the press might hover a bit now. I should have put more thought into it. I knew there was a possibility of the question coming up, but I was just planning on saying some shit about waiting for that one girl who just really got me, or whatever, you know. But the idea of anyone else thinking they could have you made me crazy and I couldn't do it."

I feel the hint of a flush coming back so I just kiss him until it fades.

"Nah," I mutter, finally. "I… Okay, at first I didn't want you to say anything, but then, I thought you denying it all would be way fucking worse. Like I was delusional in thinking this was really happening."

He snorts lightly, tugging my bottom lip with his teeth. "Oh, sugar, this is most definitely happening. Whatcha listening to?" He walks past me into the room, glances at my computer screen, and scrunches up his face. "Blech. Hipster shit."

I shake my head. "Are you kidding? This album is—"

"Conceited indie garbage," he affirms, snapping my laptop closed and walking me backwards, fingers hooked into the top of my jeans, mouth easing against mine.

"As opposed to what? The conceited non-indie garbage that we produce?" I argue, but I am distracted by the feel of his tongue sending lazy flicks against mine.

"Shut up," he instructs benignly, fingers shoving gently against my chest to indicate where he wants me.

I half-willingly stumble down on the hotel sofa, letting him straddle my thighs. I don't stop myself from touching him, my hands firm against the denim now stretched tight over his lean quads. He half drapes, half falls over me, hands bookending my head.

"Hey," he says, so gorgeous with a crooked, languid grin.

"Hi…" I answer.

"Mm." He kisses me again. "Don't talk."

"You started it," I protest, but his lips are hot against mine, and not exactly soft.

We're going at this pretty hard now, and the hint of stubble—dark blond, not black: another one of those secrets I get to know—is scraping my face. I am going to be all chafey and red, but I know I like that. Like feeling his marks on me even when he's gone. He shifts, leaning his forearm onto my chest, and kissing me harder. His other hand is tugging at the neck of my t-shirt, dragging it down angularly, and exposing my clavicle to the air. He skims it with his fingertips, breaks away to kiss it.

I emit a startled sound at the contrast of his smooth lips and rough chin against my skin, and I swear it makes him growl. He reattaches himself to my lips, and I press up into him, encouraging. I'm learning the specific taste and feel of his tongue, and I love that it is almost familiar to me now.

In response, he shifts upwards slightly, leveraging himself even more fully above me, shoving my head back into the cushion, his tongue full-out assaulting my mouth now, groping deeply, impatient. He flits it over my hard palate, a stripe then a spiral, and my body reacts for me, hips jerking upwards. He grinds down in answer.

His mouth is gone from mine, leaving me panting, just as his hand shifts strategies and races up under my shirt, fingers curious, exploring my abs, my ribs. My pec. My nipple. His fingers encircle it, closing in from all sides, and then give a questioning tug. He's watching my face, smirking as I clench my eyelids, my nipple and dick hard. Permission granted, he teases at it for a moment longer as I bite my lip and arch into the sensation.

He fastens his mouth to my jaw before dragging downwards, over my neck, and I'm gasping, jerking, needing. He's sucking now, teeth tight against the thin skin beside my Adam's apple, and I can just feel it, a small, dark, and intense hickey, and I should care. Should tell him to knock it the fuck off, but he's got both his hands up under my shirt, just touching me. The only thing that comes out is his name and not an admonishment at all. I know as soon as he pulls his face away from my neck, my shirt will be coming off. I curl upwards awkwardly, just enough for him to shuck it up over my head and arms.

"You, too," I grunt, and extend a bare arm to unzip his soft, faded hoodie.

He bats my hand away, instead choosing to yank it, along with his t-shirt, off, flinging it on the floor before bringing our naked chests hard against each other. I go to touch him, almost desperate for it, but he seizes my hands, shoving them into the couch above my head.

Arms gone, it's just torso to torso and covered cock to covered cock. Keeping both my hands gripped in one of his, he travels the other palm down my body, over my breastbone, my stomach. For a moment, he fingers the trail of hair beneath my belly button, before knuckling my hip bone for a second. I can't take it, I thrust upwards. He finally unbuttons the top of my pants.

He breaks our kiss and looks at me. I'm prostrate here. He's staring into my eyes, I'm painfully aroused, and his hands have stopped all motion.

"You sure?" he asks his tone all faux innocence, like a guy about to pop a cherry. "I mean, we won't do anything if you're not ready." Like the asshole hasn't seen me come a dozen times.

"Are you fucking *kidding* me!" I erupt, my voice high and whiny with need.

Dagen hoots with laughter, like he might just be God's gift to comedy, then unbuttons the button and unzips the zipper. He yanks at the fabric as I shimmy my hips enough to free my ass and pelvis. He bundles everything up in an unappealing package near my knees, too lazy to crawl off me to finish the job.

He palms my dick oh-so-gently, gazing at me with big, laughing eyes. He whispers sweetly, "Like that, baby? I don't wanna go too rough…"

"I am gonna fucking kill you," I mutter, my jaw clenched. I attempt to buck my hips again to increase the pressure, but he aborts the gesture, pushing down on me with the flats of his hands.

"Shush," he murmurs, petting me gormlessly. "Let me take care of you." God, he is fucking milking this prank like it is a stroke of sure genius.

"You are unbelievable," I grouse, and I know I'm being pissy, but seriously. Realizing my hands are now free, I bring them up to his shoulders, half considering just shoving him to the floor and going to the bathroom to jerk off, but he hooks his feet around my thighs and leans into me, nipping my bottom lip.

"Sorry." He grins, kissing me and not seeming particularly sorry. "Sorry, Benji," His hand winds around my cock, fingers firm. "You're just so easy." I roll my hips tentatively, to see if he is still just fucking with me. He gives my cock a sure squeeze and kisses me again. "I'll quit it, I promise. I'll be good."

He crawls backwards down my legs until he's perched over my knees. He drops down again and brings his head in towards me. He kisses my belly. One hand slips between my thighs to tease my balls, and I groan. We haven't actually done this yet, opting instead to rut against each other and bring each other off using our hands. For some reason, I thought it might be weird, because it's Dagen and he is my best friend and, like, I know he *gives* blow jobs, but knowing and seeing are two very different things.

Seeing him here, though, mouth a whisper away from my cock, I know all my stupid worrying was for nothing. He slants his eyes up at me through his dark lashes. The position of his fingers, his easy poise, the moisture-tinged heat bursting from his easily parted lips—it all oozes slutty confidence, and I feel dumb and naïve before him. He positions the plumpness of his lower lip below the ridge of my cock, like it's something precious, like his mouth is a ring-bearer's pillow. I feel ridiculous, and his eyes flash with his own brand of narcissism. He is toying with me again. It oddly makes this easier: knowing whatever we're falling into isn't unweaving the particular creation that is Dagen.

His lips close around my cock and he's all I can look at, and God help me, he looks fucking perfect.

He feels perfect, too. His mouth is warm and adept. He doesn't try to deep-throat me right off the bat, doesn't bob furiously like the myriad of porn-emulating fans who have been here before him. The suction is intense, and I can't keep still, groaning and raising my hips towards him, mouth hanging open in stupid, baffled pleasure.

"Jesus, Dag," I whisper.

He releases me with a satisfying pop, his lips redder than red, and he looks up at me with an air of self-contentment. He kisses the head of my cock cutely.

"Can I finger you?" he asks, schooling his voice into nonchalance. Like he could really go either way, and I appreciate his attempt to keep the stakes low. The offer makes me bite my lip with want. A few I've hooked up with have gone there, and the combination of a finger on my prostate and my cock in a tight throat is probably one of my favourite things ever. I've never up and asked anyone for it, though. Part of me still clings to hetero insecurities and bullshit when it comes to butt stuff, and Dag has never brought it up until now. I am fucking relieved he waited until the heat of it all, when I can have it without any awkward conversation.

"Yeah," I grunt, and his face lights up. I shift my thighs apart, trying not to look like I want it as badly as I do, and I shuffle down the couch, tilting my pelvis helpfully. He makes a show of sucking his long third finger into his mouth before letting a fat string of spit fall between my ass cheeks. He massages the ridges of my hole with the wet, warm fingertip and takes my cock in his mouth again. He takes care in entering me, and while the sensation is still slightly foreign, I appreciate the slimness of his finger and the shortness of his nail. I huff quietly, feeling my balls tighten up closer to my cock. He hums happily around my cock, and I all but manhandle his head, gripping his hair and pushing my hips up into him. His finger is deeper in my ass now, curling and seeking.

I bleat pathetically when he finds my prostate. My eyes are screwed shut, my entire existence narrowed to the staggering intensity inside me.

"Dag," I beg mindlessly, "please, Dag, right there."

He sucks at me with increased focus, fingertip pinging over the gland and making me writhe.

"Dag, shit, I'm close, I'm gonna—"

He doesn't seem fazed by my admission, and I let myself go, coming hard as he flattens his solid finger against my prostate for one long moment. I spurt off in his mouth three, four, five times, and his lips stay sealed, throat muscles spasming greedily around my cock.

I lie there panting, barely aware, as Dagen carefully withdraws his hands from my body and yanks down his jeans, crouching over me and jerking his cock frantically as his eyes bore into the flushed flesh of my chest and face and my momentarily still-hard cock. His forehead falls to my shoulder, and he grunts out a harsh sound before shooting off onto my stomach.

I think I'm losing consciousness, so tired and fucking glowing, or something, I swear. Dagen kisses my shoulder idly, shifting over a bit so he's only half on top of me and collapsing.

"Jesus, Dag, I—"

"Want to bear my children?" he suggests. "I suppose we can work something out."

"Fuck you," I say, without even a hope for conviction. I think about raising my arm to smack the back of his head, but I think we both know that is not going to happen.

"Mm. Sleep, Benji, you're slurring."

"Gonna get cum all over the couch," I reply.

He huffs but stands and pads to the bathroom, coming back with a white hotel towel. He wipes up his mess.

"Bed," he directs.

I don't argue.

Chapter Twelve

L ILLIAN AND I meet up to exchange Christmas gifts. I'm tired and a little jet lagged from the quick trip to NYC. Winter has been mild so far, but, thanks to Dagen and his stupid mouth, I'm wearing the quasi-collar of my navy blue fleece zipped up over a black hickey.

Lillian figures me out pretty quick.

"Ha!" she laughs as soon as she sees me, and reaches to unzip. "Whatcha hiding there, Ben?"

I escape her flapping hands and tug the zipper back up. "You caught me," I grumble, but I can't find it in myself to be all that pissed about it. "Before anything, I need to warn you about something," I inform her.

"Sounds serious." Her thick eyebrows arch almost all the way up to her wool hat.

"No, not really. Just this stupid interview thing—did you watch it?"

"Was I supposed to?"

"No, God no, you have a life. Just don't want to repeat the whole thing if you happened to see it. Basically, Dagen blurted out that I am seeing someone—"

"So you *are* seeing someone now? And Dagen gets to know and I don't?" Lillian exclaims, trying to act fake hurt, but I think she is a little actually hurt, too.

"We'll get to that in a minute," I promise. "But just wanted to let you know that there is a chance you and me might end up on the cover of a magazine. I mean, the press is usually pretty manageable around here, but it could happen, you know? So. Just a heads up. Tell Radley I promise I am not making a move on you or anything."

Lillian snorts. "Radley is the least jealous man I have ever met, but I will keep it in mind."

"Cool. Thanks. And I hope you don't get creepy hate mail, but it could happen and I am sorry."

"Manic, grief-stricken fan girls," Lillian deadpans. "Awesome. Now, spill, hickey-boy." She's grinning, and we leave the cafe with our drinks.

"Yeahhhh," I reply, blushing.

"You never let me give you hickeys. I'm just saying."

"And out of everything, that is what you choose to be mad about?" I jibe.

She laughs. "I think I'll live."

I shrug. "I dunno. They're embarrassing. Juvenile."

"So why'd you let mystery celeb give you one?"

"Less let."

She quirks her head.

"He had me pinned down," I mutter into the plastic lid of my coffee cup.

Her eyes grow wide and she chuckles. "Submissive much, Ben? You're just full of surprises today."

"Oh, fuck you," I grumble.

"Hey, no judgement," she assures me with a broad, over-earnest grin.

"Oh, come on! It's not like I'm harbouring fantasies of being dominated. It is just. Different. Yeah, it's different."

"Fair enough," Lillian lets it go. "You never really were all that into leather."

I snort bitterly. "Fucking Kell doesn't seem to care about that. I had to wear the tightest fucking leather pants for a shoot before the tour. Thought my sack was gonna shrivel up from dehydration."

"I know," Lillian replies smoothly. "I have a scrapbook."

"You serious?" I'm horrified.

She laughs. "Hell, no. I thought we both just agreed that I have a life. I did see that spread, though. You remember Agnieszka from senior high? She's in a couple of my courses at school and she showed it to me. Sometimes the fact that I actually know you really is surreal. Didn't stop me from laughing at your misery."

"Sadist."

"Thought you were into that?" she asks, sweetly.

"Ugh," I pout. "No."

"Fine, fine," she retreats. "I'll believe you...assuming you spill your guts to me in a satisfactory manner. This hickey means your not-really-relationship has become a really-relationship?"

"Uh. Yeah, actually. A few weeks now."

"So exciting!" She whoops, and then her tone shifts dramatically. "Oh my god, does Dagen know?"

The question confuses me for a second, like...of course Dag knows. Then the whole it's-a-big-secret thing hits me, and I stumble over a few useless vowels.

"Uhhh," I try.

Luckily, Lillian is both full of opinions and likes to talk, so looks like I won't have to reply to this one.

"Because if he doesn't, totally don't let him see this." She pokes me hard beside my Adam's apple.

"Ow!" I swat her hand away again. "And what the hell do you mean?"

She looks at me like maybe I'm half idiot.

"Uh...Benjamin?" Like she can't believe I'm actually serious.

"Uh...Lillian?" I echo facetiously.

She shifts a little awkwardly. "Nothing. Just... You know how he gets. Like psycho-possessive weird. I mean, when we got engaged, he cornered me and told me that I was a manipulative harpy hell bent on destroying your life."

"Jesus. I'm sorry. I don't understand why he gets like that around you."

"He's an asshole," she states plainly.

Yeah. He can be. My brain has been telling me this since we started this whole thing. But it still kinda stings to have someone else point it out. Besides, he hasn't been an asshole to me. Yet.

"To you. But you were kind of a bitch right back." I grimace, knowing how defensive I sound.

"Hey, a girl has her pride! And honestly, Ben? For a while, I thought it was just me, but thinking back, I'm not sure that's even true. I think it has a lot more to do with you and him than me. Like, when has he let anyone else get close to you?"

"I don't even know what you're talking about," I mumble.

She sighs tiredly. "It's just *you*. Dagen has a weird thing about you. He gets jealous of everyone. He's terrified someone else is gonna steal away his best friend, which is bizarre, considering how easily the guy makes friends. Like, he's allowed all the friends he wants, but God forbid you meet anyone new. Or if you do, he quickly whisks them away and trains them in temporary Dagen-disciple-hood. Which isn't your fault. He's just...flashier than you. He reminds me of—this sounds awful, but kind of—of a psychopath? All that charisma? If it weren't for the part where he honestly cares about you, I'd seriously question if he had any true human emotions. But he does, so." She shrugs.

"Jesus, you make him sound like some controlling creep," I argue.

"Not controlling," she amends. "I don't think it is that malicious. Just...attached, even overprotective, maybe, in a fucked-up sort of way. Like, remember Kayley Ronsky's party, seventh grade?"

I give her a blank look.

"Oh, God! I have no idea why my brain insists on remembering this shit."

"What shit?"

"Inconsequential moments at mid-puberty boy-girl parties."
She sighs. "I guess Kayley's party sticks out because I was
nervous—it was the first time I ever played, like, Spin the Bottle
and Seven Minutes and all that, you know? I was pretty sheltered."

"Okay...sounds vaguely familiar," I concede. "I didn't go to a
whole lot of those, either, I don't think."

"Because Dagen wouldn't let you." She snorts, almost under
her breath.

"What do you mean?" I demand. She ignores me, returning
to her anecdote.

"You seriously don't remember? You and Christy-Mae
Humphreys were in the closet?"

"Okay, I think I remember? Maybe?"

"Not too much to remember, because just before you were
about to embark on your seven minutes—which would have
pretty much made Christy's year, by the way, she was so into
you—"

"She was?" News to me.

"Yes, of course she was," Lillian informs me, "but that's not
the point. Before you two could really get down to it, Dagen
threw a fucking fit. About, like...nothing. We couldn't even tell
what he was going on about. All of the sudden, he just got all
pissy and said the party sucked and he wanted to go home. He
said we were all a bunch of pathetic losers, and if we wanted it so
bad, why didn't we just go out and get some—he had that eighth-
grade girlfriend for, like, a month, then, remember? He'd lost
his V-card and everyone had to fucking hear about it—and he
marched up to the closet door, threw it open, and dragged you
out. You seriously don't remember that?"

Wisps of the memory bubble to mind. I had been embarrassed,
but also kind of relieved. I hadn't kissed barely anyone back
then, and I was much happier back in Dagen's basement playing
GoldenEye on his Nintendo 64 and listening to him tell me about
what fucking was really like with masochistic interest.

"Okay, yeah," I admit. "I sort of remember that. But…uh, that was seventh grade, Lils. Doesn't exactly prove anything."

Lillian tosses her head like a frustrated pony. "And you think the way he treated me was just coincidence? He gets so fucking jealous when it comes to you, treats you like his fucking territory." She sighs, and her tirade seems to come to an end. Her voice softens. "And I get it, you know? I didn't want anyone else to have you, either, once upon a time. Because you're good, Benj, and you're…" she mulls over her next words, "careful with the people you love. A little crusty, maybe, but everyone knows that's just an act. But wanting you like that, that blindly and solely? That's being sixteen. That's the sort of shit you're supposed to grow out of."

I'm quiet, sifting through this heaviness Lillian has just poured over me. I feel kind of obtuse, having not picked up on it earlier. Like, how long has this been going on without me noticing? I'm positive that Dag never tried to hit on me pre-Allusion's success. And then we were suddenly stuck together and it just sort of happened.

Of all things, my mother's voice pops into my head. "What changed, Benjamin?" That was one of her choice phrases, growing up, any time I was pissed—or hurt, but unwilling to admit that— at the way someone was acting. Having psychologists for parents results in a lot of thought exercises. "Why do you think they thought this time they could act the way they are acting?" she would ask.

Dagen was the centre of this conversation a lot of the time, growing up. He was always getting randomly malicious with me, dramatic as he was, and leaving me stunned and wounded. My mom and I would talk it through like this, but the end result was always the same. Approaching Dagen with a lot of "I statements" and telling him he had hurt my feelings and regurgitating what my mother said about constructive arguments. By the time I was brave enough to confront him, he was usually over whatever he was mad about anyway, impatient to get on to the next adventure, the next R-movie, the next chorus.

So what changed? I seriously never even considered the idea that Dagen had had *feelings* for me before any of this started. I kinda figured he got bored and I looked, somehow, like the most challenging target around, and he thought, *sure, let's give it a whirl.*

If Lillian is right—Jesus. If Dagen has held some sort of claim to me since we were kids, if maybe it had been more than friendship for longer—much longer—than I thought, what the fuck changed? Why did he kiss me, why date me, why fuck me, and why *then*?

It's not that hard to figure out, really. On tour, I couldn't exactly run away. So he could...test the waters, see how I responded. Flirt and touch and nudge my boundaries. If I'd been really pissed, really weirded out, told him to cut it out and actually meant it, there would have been time for him to backtrack, repair things, before I could escape. And he probably didn't try anything on our first tour because he didn't want to risk the band, just in case. We're successful now; it would be much harder for me to walk away.

Half of me believes this. The other half protests that Dagen never really gave any thought to being with me until that night that Doug got sick. My mother's advice would be to stop conjecturing and just talk to him.

Bet that would go over well. I can picture it now.

Me: *So, about how long have you been in love with me?*

Dagen: *What the fuck? I'm not in love with you. Just seeing if I could get you or not. Level up my seduction xp. Turns out I could, so thanks for that.*

Me: ...

Okay, so, it might not go exactly like that. He would probably try to be all sarcastic, like, "Oh, Benji, I've always loved you,

you make me complete! I've written pages and pages in my emo diary!"

This is the definition of a useless thought exercise, because for once, I am actually sucking at gauging Dagen's possible reactions. I just wish I could tell if he was being earnest or not. I mean, I always think he is, but I've seen so many other people think that he's being serious, and they get so happy, because a Dagen high is the best feeling imaginable, I swear, and...he's not. Well, he is. For a little while. Him and his people crushes. The brief, bright few days or weeks, or occasionally months when it is all about them, them and Dagen, and all the coolhilariouswild shit they get into. But they don't last.

I barely even register it anymore, because I know his eventual destination is back on my couch, their name erased from his vocabulary as if they never existed, or replaced by another shiny human. But he always comes back. But then again, he always leaves. He needs the gloss and shine of cool: a haughtiness and inclusivity that I don't have, and don't particularly covet. But what the fuck does that all mean? Offering him an intermission from the gloss, a respite from the drugs and glory, and maybe, apparently, a place to come to, to get a little bit of care? Is that enough?

I grimace outwardly at my shitty stream of consciousness, and Lillian tilts her head and asks, "So...is it going alright then?"

"Huh?"

"The...boyfriend," she clarifies, "Or guy. The dating thing. What are you calling it, anyways?"

"Uh. Seeing? Maybe? Seeing each other? Is that a thing?" I shrug. "I dunno, but it's...good." And I mean it. It is. He's good. I'm good. We're good. Or, it was good until my sudden schizophrenic rush of doubt. Honestly. Self-esteem. I have it, my parents made sure. Just. God. I'm useless.

"Oh, yeah? Good, eh? Very, uh, descript."

118

I elbow her gently. "Shut up, Jesus, I'm not one of your girlfriends."

"Do you maybe want to rephrase that?" Her voice is still friendly but with a slight edge, and I know I'm being called out. And I also know, my mother and father being the unapologetic feminists that they are, that I should know better. "Sorry," I reply. "Sorry, I shouldn't stereotype. I'm not one of those *people* who is great with…" I look at her helplessly.

"Feelings," she finishes for me. "Oh, believe me, I know. Let's talk about our feelings, Benj…" she reiterates, mocking her younger self. She tried that line, honest to God. Repeatedly. I was in fucking eleventh grade, and she wanted me to talk about my feelings. I loved her, I really did. I just…well, I never knew what she wanted me to say. It felt like a trap and I felt like a disappointment.

"I still can't believe you pulled that on me," I accuse, gently.

"I know, I know." She hangs her head in mock-shame. "I was the actual worst." She shifts into her Benjamin-imitation mode, all shuffly and hands in pockets and chin on collarbone. "Uh, well, uh…I love you…and…uh. I really like you and…" she trails off. Pretty damn accurate.

"Ouch." I laugh.

"Okay, so, I won't make you talk about your feelings. Too much. But come on, don't you wanna gush just a little bit? Get out all the warm fuzzies that come with a new relationship?"

I kinda do want to expose all that excited disbelief curling in my abdomen, but I have no idea what to say. "I guess," I offer.

"Hmmm." She looks thoughtful. "Is he a good kisser?"

That I can answer. "Yeah."

She raises her eyebrows, smiling. "You gonna elaborate on that?"

I shake my head at her. "You're incorrigible. Uhhh. Hard. He kisses hard, and I like it. Like, he is demanding my attention and I better fucking give it to him."

She eyes my neck amusedly. "I got that much." She pauses, thinking again. "You always did like needy," she says with good humoured self-depreciation. "And...does he...buy you lots of nice stuff?"

I look at her confusedly.

"Kidding. I know, you live like a Spartan. Fuck. You are making this way difficult! Maybe girls—shit, maybe some *people*—are just better at spilling. 'Chelle tells me stuff I don't even want to know, half the time. Once she gave me a description of her shit. Like, her literal shit. She was on this ridiculous fad cleanse that was all about interpreting your BMs, and it was awful. I can never see her the same way again."

"You want me to tell you stuff you don't want to know?" I ask skeptically.

"I don't know!" Lillian whines. "I just want to have a gossipy gush sesh."

I cringe at the abbreviation. "Well...I suck at those."

"Yeah, obviously," she agrees. There's a beat and then she apparently decides to just go for it. "Are you sleeping with him?"

"Yeah...?" I answer hesitantly, "I mean, I guess it depends on what you count as sex."

"So no anal," she elucidates, all matter-of-fact.

"Christ, Lillian," I sigh, shaking my head.

"You don't have to answer. I'm sorry. I'm nosy. I took this healthy sexuality course and we talked a lot about the harms of *not* talking about sex, and the stigma that creates. But we also talked about boundaries. And I'm obviously trampling all over yours, so, I'm sorry. We can change the subject." There is a bit of pomposity in her lecture that makes me smile.

"College is really doing it for you, hey?" I rib.

She laughs. "Can't help myself. But yeah. It is. I love it. Some days I feel like my brain is literally expanding. Like...there are so many thoughts that I have never even thought of having. I was pissed about having to take non-bio electives, but I am glad I did now. I mean, just the sex course alone kinda revolutionized things for me. All these preconceived notions I had about sexuality and sex work and intersections between age and sex and—it is incredible, everything is just so turned around and it feels good, you know? Like, if I'd had the baby and married you—I would be the same person now that I was then. Just more tired and way more bitter. I gave myself a second chance, and I'm not wasting it, and I'm *happy*." She beams at me and I can't help but hug her.

"Good," I tell her. "I don't know what all the words you just said mean, but God knows, I'm glad for you, Lils."

She hums and breaks free of the hug. "But anyway, I have learned to be a lot more open and relaxed about sex, and so have a lot of my friends, so I forget not everyone wants me prying. I just think sex is so interesting and people are interesting. But I'm sorry," she repeats.

"No, it's...fine." And it is fine. It isn't like I haven't talked about fucking a million times before with Dagen or Luce or other guys from high school, admittedly in less Lillian-approved ways, but still. "No, we haven't tried...that."

"Are you going to?" she inquires. "Tell me to shut it at anytime."

I suddenly understood what Lillian meant about having her brain stretched. I hadn't even thought about it like that. I thought it was an eventuality, not an option. Like...if Dag wasn't eventually getting some, or vice versa, did it count as a relationship?

"Probably."

"Cool. Radley and I have tried it a few times. Both ways. It is actually kind of fun."

I try not to start. "Oh!"

"Sorry," she apologizes for the millionth time. "Too much?"

"No, it's cool," I reply. "Just wasn't expecting that. But, yeah. I—I want to. I think. It just hasn't happened. I mean, fingers, yeah, but not anything else."

"Does it freak you out?"

"I don't know. I don't think so. I mean, I've read enough *Savage Love* to have some idea of how it all works. But it'll be awkward, and what if I don't like it or he doesn't or we don't want it the same way. Fuck. Blow jobs are just so much easier."

"Wow. Sounds like the communication thing is really happening for you," she replies sarcastically. "Did you at least take the good columnist's advice and lay your kink cards on the table?"

"I don't think I really have any kink cards. I like fucking. I like him. I like fucking him, at least, the version of it we are engaging in. He likes...he really likes to dirty talk. I thought that would make me uncomfortable, but when I'm in it with him, hearing all this obscene shit, I like that. Except I can't tell if he actually wants to do that stuff, or if he just likes talking about it."

"You could try asking," Lillian suggests, not at all helpfully.

"Thanks, Tips," I reply drily, then sigh. "No, you're right. And I think I will. Eventually. Just not...yet. And I think I'm ready for that subject change now."

She laughs. "I'm not surprised. That is more sharing than you did in our entire relationship."

"Here." I thrust an envelope at her. "Christmas." I explain.

She takes it from me curiously. I just got her some concert tickets, nothing that exciting.

"Oh my god! The New Pornographers? Are you serious, Benjamin? THANK YOU SO MUCH! I'LL TOTALLY TAKE YOU!"

Guess it's a bit more exciting than I thought.

"I'm going already. Hence the two. Take Radley or someone."

"Okay," she nods, "I will. Seriously. Thanks, Ben, this is...wow. I was so pissed because I forgot to buy tickets and they sold out so fast because of the intimate venue and I was kicking myself. This is perfect. You're the best."

I shrug bashfully. "Don't worry about it, uh...Merry Christmas, or whatever."

She smiles, really sincerely, and gives me a hug. "Thank you, Ben, really. And…I got you something, too…but you'll be mad…"

I eye her apprehensively. "I'll be mad?"

She sheepishly hands me a little brown paper bag. "I wanna explain first, like, before you open it. I figured if you and, uh, mystery guy, are trying to keep this whole thing a secret, because, like, you're both famous, and you haven't spilt yet as to just how famous we are talking here…well, someone might notice you. So, I thought I would pick it up for you, so you didn't have to…" She trails off, and my curiosity is beyond piqued.

I start to unfurl the softly rumbled edges of the bag, when she starts up again.

"Shit. Now I am embarrassed. When I bought it, I was so proud of myself and now I feel stupid." She bites her lip and scrunches up her face, obviously just wanting to get this over with.

There is some weight to the gift, and I look inside the bag to see a round, red plastic bottle. I turn it until the label is in view. *Getting Physical*, it reads in a cheeky font, and underneath, in much smaller lettering, *thin-coat, water-based personal lubricant*. I fumble the bottle like it's hot to the touch, and it plops back into the bag.

"You…you got me lube?" I stare at Lillian, in half horror, watching her brown cheeks flush.

"Uh. Yeah?" She grimaces. "I thought it would be quirky and fun, but now I am just feeling like a creep." Her uncertainty gives the ends of her sentences upward inflection as she babbles on. "It's a good brand, though? I. Um. I did research? And I checked with the clerk." The words topple over each other as she rushes to get them out.

I don't know what to say. She's not wrong. Not that a straight guy can't buy lube, but most straight guys don't have the semi-distant threat of the press over them, hoping to catch them doing something banal enough for a "They're Just Like US" segment. I can see it now: "Dagen Mercutio cares about his partner's comfort, just like US!" I cringe at the thought and raise my eyes to meet Lillian's.

"Thanks, Lils. This is actually incredibly considerate of you." I smile. "Creepy, but considerate."

She bites on her lip for a second, then blurts out, "And it's water-based, so it won't denigrate the condoms. You're using condoms, right?"

"Uh. Not for what we've done so far."

Lillian sighs and shakes her head and goes straight into lecture mode. "I know oral doesn't necessarily seem like sex, but you can still catch STIs from it, so you should be being tested *and* using a condom until you decide to be exclusive." She rattles off. "You've at least been, tested, right?"

I give her a guilty look and fortify myself for another sermon.

Chapter Thirteen

W HEN I GET home a few hours later, Dagen is in my kitchen. I skulk in, tired and feeling dumb. Lillian's admonishments were both annoying, and, regretfully, completely deserved. I unload my canvas messenger bag on the breakfast bar. Dagen's steaming wraps over the kettle.

"You do remember that you don't actually live here, right?" I ask.

"Hmm," Dagen answers, noncommittally.

"You're not paying rent, for example," I continue. But I know that's lame, because he totally would pay rent except that I won't let him pay rent because that would mean that he lives here when I'm trying to enforce that he doesn't. Useless, I know.

He doesn't even argue with me. Just gives me a half-smile. "I'm making fajitas," he says instead.

"With what?" is my only response.

"I shop!" Dagen protests. Which we both know is only true about ten percent of the time.

I ignore him and go to take a piss. The bathroom counter is cluttered with his razor and deodorant, and little brown stubbly hairs are scattered in the sink like little insects. The cap is off the toothpaste. I almost trip over his wet towel.

I look around, unimpressed. I swear I cleaned up only this morning.

"Dagen! If you're going to pretend to live here, fucking clean up after yourself!" I grouse.

"Sorry!" he shouts back, completely affable, and why is it so fucking hard to fight with someone when they are determined to be pleasant. I kick the towel to the side of the floor and recap the Crest. Jesus, when did he fucking move in, anyway? The answer my brain provides me with is surprising. He moved in sometime after my divorce and he just never left. We've just been touring, and he still keeps lots of shit at Miranda's so I didn't quite notice.

He's been crashing with me semi-constantly since we were kids—whenever my parents would let him. So weekends, mostly. And when I moved out, he basically just moved with me, crashing on the couch more nights than not, blaming public transit for not running late enough. And now he's sleeping in my bed and not on the couch and is cooking in my kitchen.

I watch him when I get back into the kitchen. He's pretty intent on his frying, rhythmically flicking his bangs off his forehead as he shuffles the chicken and onions around the pan with my silicone spatula. He scrapes the peppers off the cutting board into the mix.

"Should be ready in a few," he says, and I nod, half stunned by the sudden domesticity. Or maybe it is less the domesticity that is sudden and more my realization of it.

I set the table. Milk for me, water for him. And I realize that Dag and I make a better married couple than Lillian and I ever did. It's so easy between us. He's not picking at me, grilling me, trying to sculpt me into some husbandly ideal. I know what he likes and he knows me, and we've been like this for a long time now. *How long?* I catch myself wondering. How long has he...wanted me, or whatever? And how come I didn't know? He catches me watching him, and smiles, relaxed, content.

"Food's up," he informs me, pouring the fillings into a big bowl and adding a servicing spoon.

I move the plate with the still-warm wraps to the table and sit down.

"Thanks," I hear myself saying.

"You're welcome," he replies.

***

Dagen's always cold, so the heat in the apartment is way up. After dinner, I go to the bedroom to change out of my fleece and into a t-shirt.

"Sugar, I'm touched," Dagen states, false-sweet, when I enter the room.

I look at him, momentarily confused, until I focus in on the bright-red container in his hand.

"Uhh," I articulate, face flushed like a sunburn. "I don't know. Just... Just in case. I guess."

Dagen plants the lube back on the bar and stalks toward me. "Mm. Just in case, hey?"

I shrug dumbly as he reaches me, his clever fingers lingering on the top edge of my jeans.

"You wanna fuck me, Benji?" he murmurs huskily, pressing into me and kissing the side of my neck. "Or are you gonna let me fuck you?"

And I can't say either idea is lacking in appeal. I keep my neck exposed for him and let myself think about it. How would I want it? It wigs me out decidedly less to think about fucking him. He's done it before, he knows he likes it, there wouldn't be any of the newness or weirdness that there is bound to be with me. I can picture him underneath me, tight little ass pushing back eagerly. The undoubtedly loud and shameless noises he'll make.

He's nuzzling my cheekbone with his nose, lips very close to mine, trying to get me to give first, but I won't. He nips at the corner of my mouth, and I respond readily, still thrilled with the press of his lips and chest and hips against mine.

"Benj..." And honestly it is a relief to hear him sound as needy as I feel. His bony-strong fingers creep up under the sides of my shirt and alight up my sides, just hard enough not to tickle. His face is so close to mine, but I can focus on pieces of him: the outline of those gorgeous eyelashes; his ear, which I can just make out through the dramatic sweep of his hair.

Things intensify quickly, and we make the awkward walk from the kitchen to the bedroom where we keep our hands off each other long enough to strip. I notice Dag put the red bottle on the dresser before he presses into me again, sucking my lower lip before nudging me back onto the bed. He kneels between my thighs like before, sucking on the head of my cock, and sometimes I still can't believe that this is a thing we do now.

He's making it messy on purpose, directing the excess saliva to my ass. I think about feeling guilty for letting him do this again, without me even having had a chance to reciprocate, but he doesn't seem to mind. I melt backwards onto my elbows and lift one foot up onto the bed. Dagen pops off my cock long enough to grin at me and grope blindly for the bottle of lube.

"This okay?" he asks, indicating the bottle.

I groan appreciative consent, and he teases a fingertip across my asshole.

"Yeah, I guess it's not like the fajitas will work their particular brand of magic just yet."

I stare at him disbelievingly, "Jesus fucking Christ, Dag. Could you maybe *not* make shit jokes when I am about to get off?"

He seems to consider it as he slides his stupid, expert finger up my ass, making me bite my lip at the feel of it all.

"I mean, I could try," he says, conversationally. "But I doubt I will succeed. Assholes and shit jokes kind of go together."

"Get your fucking mouth back on my cock before you completely destroy the mood," I groan, and Dagen, thankfully, acquiesces.

***

He gets me off. Swallows my load like it is no big thing—another favour I'm not sure I'll be able to return, at least, not smoothly. After I've come, though, he keeps his finger inside of me—reducing the friction on my prostate and just teasing the rim, carefully adding another finger and marking my reaction.

"What do you think?" he asks, and I claw my way back to consciousness enough to interpret what he is asking. "Do you wanna try?"

I notice that the hand that is not currently working my asshole is gripped comfortably around his cock and yes, I do want to try. I want to have the chance to make him feel at least half as good as I feel, and I almost catch myself nodding.

"Yeah," I say cautiously. "I do want to try. I just..." I swallow. I hate this. Why does being responsible have to so inconvenient? "I think we should get tested, first. I mean, we could just do it right now. I think I still have some condoms kicking around, but I dunno. I kind of hate condoms—I mean you know I use them, but they kind of suck, and I would...kind of rather...not. But we should get tested first. Because we kind of get around."

"Fine, fine," Dagen says, climbing from the floor to the bed. "Fuck. I mean, you're right, but talk about timing, Jesus."

"I know," I reply. "I'm sorry, it sucks. I wasn't planning—"

"Please stop talking," Dagen says, smiling. "We can talk all you want, but for the love of Christ, can I get off first?"

"Yes," I reply, sheepishly. "Definitely. Sorry."

His mouth closes on mine, and I reach between us, replacing his hand on his cock with mine.

"Bit tighter," he instructs throatily. "Fuck. Yeah. That."

The angle is kind of off, and I'm definitely not used to this, but I'm greedy for the feel and sight of him. He presses his forehead into my shoulder as his breathing becomes haggard.

"Fuck, sweets—fuck, so good..." And then he is shooting off onto my chest and stomach with a satisfied groan and I find myself feeling bizarrely proud.

***

So we go to the lab and do the whole piss-in-a-cup thing. Some blood is drawn and some insurance papers are signed and we're told to check back in 7–10 business days if we don't hear anything sooner, and I am thinking that is it. And then, a few days later, while I am breaking in a new-ish Destroyer album, and Dagen is perfecting his Wii golf swing, his phone goes off.

I'm a nosy, slightly *jealous even if I don't want to admit it* asshole, so, of course, I pause the CD and come out into the living room to very obviously eavesdrop. There's not much to listen in on.

"Oh, hi." A pause. "Oh. Okay, can you— No, no, yeah, for sure." Another pause. "Yep, I'll come by later today. Thanks."

He hangs up the phone.

"What was that about?" I ask, aiming for and missing nonchalance.

"Clinic," he says. "They say I have to follow up with them. Right away."

It is like a trap door opens below me. I'm stumbling on solid ground. Except I'm not stumbling, I still. Frozen. "Did they say what..."

"They can't. Phone confidentiality and shit."

"Oh," I reply flatly. "Right."

"They said they can sneak me in later today."

"Oh. That's good, then." Is it? Or does that mean it is extra bad. Jesus.

Dagen tosses his head and opens his mouth. Closes it again. Sighs. "Fuck," he says.

"Yeah," I agree.

"Will you..." he starts, sighs again. "Will you go with me?" The panic filters out of me slowly, fading to dull worry. I step close.

"Of course I will."

***

Having not spent a lot of my life sick, I'm not exactly used to clinic waiting rooms. The posters about vaccinations and symptoms of sleep apnoea and the muted colours do nothing to divert the fact that everyone waiting here is sick. Sick and waiting. And stressed.

Dag and I are stressed. And waiting. And Dagen might even be sick.

A woman in scrubs mispronounces Dagen's name. We both stand without correcting her and follow her down a hallway with pot lighting and pictures of sailboats, into an exam room. The roll-out paper crinkles as Dagen sits on the exam table. I think about sitting on the chair, but I can't just now. I wanna be close to him. Within touching distance. Even though we are not out, and even though I don't even know if he wants me to touch him, and even though we are steeling ourselves for the worst and maybe we'll come out the other side beyond reach.

A doctor enters and tells us his name, which I forget immediately. I sit in the chair because I feel like I am taking up too much room; it suddenly feels fucking weird for two grown-ass men to be in an exam room together.

The doctor pulls the wheelie stool under him and opens the too-white stock paper chart. It's all very surreal. And I just know that it's not gonna be good news.

***

"Gonorrhoea, Dagen, seriously?" I mutter beneath my breath as we exit the clinic, prescriptions in hand. Because apparently, even if I didn't test positively for it, I have to be treated, too. Because oral gonorrhoea is apparently a thing. Jesus fucking Christ.

"I'm sorry, Benj," he says. "I swear to God, I had no idea."

"I know," I sigh. "I know you didn't. And I know we should've been tested before we started all this. Fuck, we should have gotten tested when the tour wrapped up and we just fucking didn't. And yeah, I'm pissed at you, but honestly, more than anything, I'm just fucking relieved."

I'm not a hand-holding guy. Even with Lillian, she had to pester me into it. But on our way out of the pharmacy, I suddenly feel like I can't help myself. I reach for him and he lets me.

I grip Dagen's hand all the way to his car, suffocating the life out of the fingers interlocked with mine. Noon-bright sun and a shitload of spectators, and I don't even fucking care.

***

"You think they'd come up with a better system," Dagen comments on the drive home. I let go of him only long enough for us to get into the car. He is driving one-handed but doesn't seem fussed. He skirts his thumb over my knuckle every couple of minutes, and I'm thankful for it. "Like, you'd think they'd at least be able to tell you on the phone whether or not you have a fucking terminal illness."

"I want to sleep with you," I answer, non-sequentially. "Once this is gone, we are fucking."

Dagen quirks me a grin. "Man, I should not get AIDS every day."

I should tell him that's not an okay joke, that if my folks had heard him, they'd be furious and disappointed, and he knows it. But I'm too wired to bother, caught somewhere between adrenalized and sick. And scared. For a second, everything had ended, and I know I don't want that.

"I wonder who I got it from," Dagen muses. "I wonder how I tell the unwashed masses. Is it totally immoral to not make an effort? Don't answer that." He drives too fast, but the shocks are quality and we're soaring. Or maybe that's just me. I don't know. I love turning corners in his car.

I shake my head to indicate that I don't have the energy for any of these questions.

"Hey," he says after a long time, squeezing my hand, "It's basically not anything."

"It could've been," I mutter.

"Everything could've been, Benji," he says, but not unkindly.

He sails into the parking spot at my building. We climb out of the car and he re-catches my hand, fingers between fingers in the elevator.

"I don't think I'm just relieved," I admit, once we're together in the apartment. Dagen stops rooting through the fridge and turns to me. "I'm definitely also pissed," I explain. "I really don't want to be, but I think I am."

Dagen sets his uncharacteristically solemn gaze on me and waits for me to continue.

"You aren't careful. I get that, I know that. I know I can fucking lecture you all I want, but you're gonna do what you're gonna do, and that is fine. But. Fuck, Dag. Seriously—this was a really shitty thing to do to me. Like, why would you chance it like that?"

Dagen slides his hands into his pockets, and it makes him look five years younger. "Because I'm a fucking idiot," he responds. "I don't have a good answer. I fucked up. I honestly just didn't even think about it." He hunches and his hair falls into his eyes. "I'm sorry. I feel like a real prick, if that helps at all."

I slump forward in my barstool and rest my forehead in my hands and feel the silence amplify between us.

Dagen edges close to me, as if waiting for permission to touch. I reach out one hand for his.

"Do you..." I pause, not sure how much of myself I should really put out there. "Do you get what this means to me?" I ask, giving in. "Us, I mean? I feel like I should, I don't know, play it cool or something. Not get attached, but I'm used to you now. I'm falling into the whole *can't picture my life without this* stuff. Not that I ever really could, but now, there is this extra layer and then we both go and do this stupid, reckless thing and—"

"Hey." Dagen's hand leaves mine to slide up my forearm, pull me in, kiss me. "You're not exactly alone in this, you know," he says with a small smile. "And I really am sorry for maybe giving you gonorrhoea."

I butt my head into his very gently and laugh. "Well, thanks."

He kisses me again before pulling back. "You know I love you, right?" he says. His tone is light, curious. Like he just now considered the possibility that I didn't know.

"Uh," I answer eloquently.

"Shit, Benji." He laughs. "Of course I fucking love you. No idea what good that does you, given that I'm ninety-nine percent selfish asshole, but even in all of that, I love you." He kisses me again, he's playful, but I'm still processing.

"Could you do me a favour, maybe?" I ask between kisses.

"Anything," he promises.

"I'm really fucking gone on you. And I am really, really hoping that…this isn't going to turn out to be some colossal mistake. So if you could maybe just not hurt me or something? That… That would be good," I finish toothlessly.

I'm quickly reassured by Dagen's very earnest-seeming lips. His tongue never even enters my mouth, and yet I somehow feel like I've never been kissed this deeply in my life, like he's found something no one could even touch before.

"Sweets," he says, steadying me when I didn't even know I wasn't steady. "I *love* you. And…I wouldn't. Do anything. And I wish I knew why you are so sure I will. At some point in your life, you're going to have to consider believing in me, at least when it comes to you."

I don't know how to answer, and we're so saturated with words that I just bring his head back towards mine and try to communicate what I don't know how to without using any words at all.

Chapter Fourteen

IT'S TIME FOR another dinner at my parents' house. Dagen, as usual, is invited along. He's been part of the family for so long that I have no idea why we didn't just start this whole thing earlier, I mean, it would've saved me a metric shit-ton of inner turmoil.

My father takes our coats in the front hall, and we congregate in the living room. My mother serves us red wine. She's a bit of a wine snob, and has been trying to similarly refine Dagen and me since we were teenagers. She has always sort of pooh-poohed the legal drinking age.

Dag and I didn't exactly talk about how we wanted to play this, and really I am not sure how to go about outing myself, so I am thinking of maybe just not, at least for now. Maybe it is self-preservation. The fewer people who know my heart is compromised, the fewer who will be aware when my heart gets broken.

"So, boys," my mother starts in with the regular pre-dinner question period, "working on new material already, or taking a bit of a breather?"

And so it begins, not interrogative, but still making sure to cover all possible aspects of both mine and Dagen's lives, getting that stuff out of the way so that we can have philosophical conversation over dinner. That's the way my mom's mind works. Stimulating conversation makes a meal taste better; dry conversation makes wine taste better. We cover the state of my apartment, Miranda's well-being, the well-being of my apartment, Lillian, our band and its progress, Doug and Luce...

"And, Dagen, when you're not writing music, how are you spending your time?"

Dagen grins at me mischievously, very quickly scanning my body with his eyes. Oh, no, he would not...

"Oh, you know, Mrs. W.," Dagen gives her his biggest shit-eating grin, still calling her that, even though he's been invited to be on a first-name basis with my folks more than once. Old habits, and all that. "I'm not doing a heck of a lot. Honing my Nintendo skills. We've got a Wii set up in the apartment, and it's addictive as hell."

My father chuckles. "Good to hear you're not growing up too fast."

"Have you tried one yet?" Dagen asks my dad. "It's really something else. You've gotta come over," Dagen continues, "Benj and I'll show you. You'll get a kick out of it."

If my parents think it is weird that Dagen just invited my dad over to my apartment, neither of them say anything. My dad just returns Dagen's grin and says he might have to do just that.

It's easy, it is small talk. I should be starting to relax, but Dagen seems to side just a little too close to me, and with psychologists for parents, I've always been hyper aware of what kind of signals I might be giving off. I try to edge away, but there is nowhere to go unless I plaster myself against the arm of the couch or move altogether. And that wouldn't look bizarre or anything. I feel my body start to heat; my neck sweats and prickles. And Dag keeps looking at me. Smiling at me, big and open, and it just screams obvious.

My parents head to the kitchen to serve dinner.

"Could you cool it?" I hiss as soon as they are out of earshot.

"Cool what?" he asks.

"This. Sitting so close to me. Looking at me like that."

His mouth twists into a self-satisfied smile. "I thought you liked being looked at like that."

"You're making me nervous. They're going to figure us out."

"So, let's just tell them," Dagen replies, like this isn't a big fucking deal.

"Tell them?!" My voice cracks like I'm thirteen.

"Yeah, tell them," he proceeds. "Sugar, why not? Your parents are my second family. They should know."

"Know, what, exactly? It's not like we've even established what's going on here. Our relationship is totally lacking in description."

His eyes widen slightly. "What's that supposed to mean?" He keeps neutral, but I can tell he's on the defensive.

"It just means that even if we did tell them, I don't know what we would tell them."

"Tell them we're seeing each other. Romantically," he says, a hint of laughter tinting his voice as he flicks his eyebrows upwards on the last word.

"Ha-fucking-ha."

He laughs. "We'll just say we're dating."

"Oh, brilliant. I can picture it now: Mom, Dad, Dagen and I are dating. Their response: Oh, really, who're the lucky ladies?"

"Good point." He sighs. "I don't know, sweets, maybe if you wanna start giving me a quick blowie, when they come in they'll get the gist. Totally save us an awkward conversation."

I give him what I hope is a scathing look, and he laughs. "Oh, come, on, Benji, it's not a big thing. Your parents are chill; they won't even bat an eye. I mean, if you have to come out to parents, yours are probably the best in the world to come out to. Besides, I hate keeping my hands off you."

"Yeah," I agree, hesitantly. "It's not like I am ashamed or anything. We're just shiny and new, and that always fades, and if we fuck this up—they'll be so disappointed. They don't want to lose you, either."

"Okay, let me just make myself clear. No matter what we are to each other, unless you send me away—and probably not even then—I'm never *not* gonna be in your life. I'm never not gonna love you. I'm always gonna be around to have dinner with your parents. Besides, you know they worry about you after the whole divorce thing. They want you to be happy."

"I am happy," I insist.

"I know. I just want them to know that I am gonna do my best to keep you that way."

I pause. "Yeah. I mean, it's not like I think they'll be mad about it."

"So you'd be okay if I told them?"

"Uh, yeah, I guess so. Save me from having to do it."

"So that's a yes?" He is strangely intense.

"Fine. Sure."

He grins warmly, "Thanks, Benji." He threads a hand through my hair, draws me in, and kisses me and I let him.

My father clears his throat.

The little shit. He saw this coming.

I spring away from Dag, thwacking my back on the arm of the couch. We look up at my dad, Dagen doing a shitty job of feigning guilt, me swimming in it.

"Paige," my father says calmly as my mother enters the living room behind him, "I think the boys have an announcement to make."

***

An hour has passed since I fumbled through an explanation to my parents. I'm pretty sure the almost painful flush in my face has come to stay permanently. Dagen, however, is anything but embarrassed. In fact, I'm not sure I've ever seen him as proud of himself as he is tonight. We're back in the living room for pre-dessert conversation, and Dagen hasn't removed his hand from my knee since we got here, the possessive bastard.

He probably knows that it is the last time I'll ever let him touch me, possibly ever, before I exterminate him with the sheer force of my embarrassed rage. Actually, he probably doesn't. He's fucking stupid when it comes to certain things. Things like kissing me, on purpose, in front of my parents.

Not that they didn't take it well. Dagen is already practically a son to them, so he might as well be a fucking prospective son-in-law. And…I know that's not why I'm mad. I know I even kind of like the way Dagen keeps contact, the way he puffs up when he talks about us.

It's just the danger of this all falling apart. If, or maybe even when, Dagen finds his new temporary best friend, I know I'll always be in the background for him, a place to return to. But what if that just makes him feel guilty or obligated? So we end things. And now my parents know, and so then they will feel obligated to try and comfort me or coddle me, and when you've got your heart scrambled, when all you want to do is burrow under your duvet and die…

"Sugar? You okay?" Oh, fucking Christ. He did not just call me that in front of my parents. I barely tolerate it when we're alone. What the actual fresh hell?

I blink.

Oh. We are alone.

"Don't call me that in front of my parents," I warn for the future.

"I won't if you don't want me to," he agrees easily.

He considers me for another moment. My parents are serving dessert.

"You gonna tell me what's wrong?"

"I don't know," I answer. "It's just…isn't this going to really suck when we break up?"

"We're breaking up?" Dag looks at me, half amused.

I sigh. "I don't know! Isn't that what couples do? Break up?"

"Yeah, I guess, some couples break up. And some couples don't. You need to calm your neurotic self down, Benji."

I collapse my head backwards onto the couch. He's right. I need to fucking stop overthinking and just enjoy the ride. I'm not usually so fucking high strung.

"Sorry." I sigh. "I just wasn't expecting all this to come out tonight."

"You're making it very hard for me to not make a pun right now."

"Well, I appreciate your efforts."

He kisses my temple.

He's cute sometimes.

***

We get back to the apartment, having escaped my parents without too many more uncomfortable questions. I take a piss and then head to the kitchen, where I throw back my last two doxycycline pills. I chuck Dagen's little blue plastic bottle at him, and he catches it. Pours the last two pills out into his palm and then looks up at me.

"Let's do this, then," I say, stripping off my hoodie.

"Huh?" Dagen replies.

"Gonorrhoea-free. I told you. I don't want to wait. I want you to fuck me."

I grip his collar and kiss him fiercely, a lot of fucking emotions finally allowing themselves to dissipate.

Dagen returns the kiss before he coaxes me back. "Benji, sugar, don't take this the wrong way. I mean…I want to fuck you. Fucking Christ, it's all I've thought about for practically ever." He's looking a little worriedly into my eyes. "But I don't think now, right this second, is the best timing in the world."

"Why not? Why not now? I could have a fucking brain aneurysm in a minute and we'll never have even gotten there."

"Whoa. Benji." He holds onto my shoulders as I try to kiss him. "Calm the fuck down, beautiful. You're all wrung out, you're not you."

"But…"

"We're not taking this any further until we're both feeling much more rational and haven't had any STD scares or out-of-the-closet announcements and it isn't wrought with all this shit. Let's just make out, get off, calm down."

I let him hug me. I collapse my head towards his, and we kiss softly. Finally, I think I'm breathing normally, thinking like myself again.

"Dag?" I whisper.

"Mm?"

"So…I promise to never have an emotional meltdown again."

He cracks up, steps back. Pours us some orange juice.

"Well, fucking good. I'm not used to being the calm and collected one, and I'm not sure I love it." He takes a sip of his juice, "I do love you, though."

I feel myself smile. "Yeah, I think you mentioned that."

"You know me. All about the excessive."

***

And so Dagen and I play Wii for a bit and have a couple of beers. I'm starting to feel a lot more glued together, and when he crawls under the duvet, I reach over to touch him. I rest my hand lightly on his chest, and he covers it with his fingers. Then, he rolls over onto his side, facing me. I inch a little closer to him, slip my hand up under his shirt along his naked hip. He kisses me easily, touching my hair as he cautiously probes my mouth. His tongue feels warm against mine, slow in its movements, as if we have forever to taste each other. He slides along my inner cheeks, skims my teeth, explores the area beneath my tongue, like he's mapping me out.

I pulse my tongue back against his and feel his retreat, and I follow him. It is such a strange concept, being allowed to feel what only he gets to feel, the tip of my tongue searching for those untouched ridges and edges. I draw back a little. He takes my lower lip between his, cocooning it, kneading it with his lips, his tongue, and I swear every nerve in my body has translocated itself to that one spot.

He pulls back. Looks at me through those fucking lashes. I greedily run my eyes over him, bringing my fingertips up to trace the miniature bones in his neck. My mouth takes over the exploration, charting the delicate structure beneath the surface. I shift my mouth, brushing just the outermost layer of my lips against his Adam's apple which bobs as he swallows, making me smile slightly. I migrate lower. The flat edge of my curled fingers skims the hollow at the base of his throat. I follow up with another kiss, which expands out, grazing over his clavicle. I flick my tongue very slightly against the bone, and Dagen murmurs, relaxing onto his back, exposing himself to me.

I slip lower beneath the duvet, my face level with his breastbone. I press my palm against his chest until I gauge his heartbeat before replacing my hand with my lips. I explore his torso this way, fingers followed by palms followed by mouth. Over his ribs, his abs, and then I nuzzle his belly button with my nose before I kiss it. Whorl my tongue around the edge, dip inside. And I hear him giggle appreciatively. His boxers ride low over his hips, and I have the bones and hollows there to discover. And then I return to his nipples. They harden beneath my touch, pert and pebbly in my mouth, and I bet they ache. That's because of me, and I like that: that tangible evidence of my presence. Finally, when I feel that I know his body quite thoroughly, I shift back up. I position my upper body above his, supporting my weight on my hands on either side of him. I kiss him fully, bent into him.

He suddenly spins us, so he's completely covering me. His hands deftly strip me of my t-shirt, and I feel his erection hard against my thigh. He kisses me deeply, tongue moving faster than before, thrusting long and deliberate. His chest presses into mine, as his hands range over my skin, gripping my shoulder blades, my back.

I want him.

I tug at the elastic of his boxers, and he quickly reacts, pushing me off him in order to strip both of us of our clothing. Then he's over me and we're tight against each other. I thrust against him, but he grips my hair and whispers into my ear.

"Wait."

I try to stop moving but it's so hard, his body hot and wanting against me. He kisses me, and then shifts, positioning himself between my legs, which I bend. His hands roam over my thighs, up my sides, then down along my butt.

"So..." He asks permission. "You know what I said before about waiting?"

"Yeah..."

"Well, I changed my mind. I think that is definitely a bullshit idea. In fact, I think right now is an absolutely perfect time to fuck."

"Funny," I reply, smiling into the skin of his shoulder, "I was just thinking the same thing."

He leans up to kiss me again, this time edging away from my mouth and running his lips over my neck, reinforcing my erection.

"That so?" he asks.

"Fuck. Yes."

"Roll over, sugar. Let me at you."

He climbs off me to go grab the lube, and I kick off the remainder of the duvet, and turn onto my front. My body is charged and ready, and I'm nervous, maybe, but not horribly so.

Dagen kisses the small of my back, coursing his knuckles down the muscles of my ass, and I groan.

"Fuck, feels good," I tell him.

"This'll feel even better," he promises, running a lubed finger between my butt cheeks.

He's not wrong. I shift up onto my knees so I can get at my cock while Dagen coaxes the ring of my ass into relaxing.

One finger feels good, familiar, but when he adds a second, the feeling changes. I remember the first time a girl went there, fingering me while she sucked me off. I remember being kind of horrified, but getting over that in a hurry when she found my p-spot.

"You good?" he asks, and I grunt yes, even if "good" might not be the way I would describe it. It feels too full, unnatural. My body wants to fight it. I force myself to relax, and Dagen considerately curls his fingers to the right angle to hit my prostate a few times, and with that, two fingers stops feeling like a big deal.

He adds a third. I hiss as all pretence of pleasure fades. I knew it would hurt, but Jesus.

"Ow. Fuck," I mutter.

"Sorry," he whispers. "Sorry, sweets. Do you want me to stop?" he asks, but my erection is still in full force, thanks to his efforts, and we're going to have to get past this one of these days.

"No," I mutter, teeth clenched. I work my dick a little more forcefully, trying to concentrate on that instead of the slight burn in my ass. He seats his fingers in me, careful not to make any sudden movements, just pulsing pleasantly on my prostate. He leans in and puts his mouth against my chode, striping his tongue along it.

I whimper a little at that. It feels good but also so fucking personal. He sucks lightly at my balls and I can't really fucking believe that this is Dagen making me feel like this, focusing his efforts on my body so completely.

"Can I?" he asks.

"Yeah." I breathe. "Go." I want to add *before I lose my nerve*, but I know that then he'll stop, and I want to do this. I'm under no illusions that it is going to be awesome. But we'll never get to awesome if we don't get through this part first.

I hear him slick himself up. He runs his cock head along my crack once or twice before pausing at the entrance.

"Tell me if it's too much and I'll stop," he assures me.

I bite my lip. "Yeah," I lie. I know I won't be stopping him. If I don't do this now, I feel like I might chicken out forever.

He carefully enters me, just the head, and I'm biting my lip so hard it almost bleeds because it fucking hurts. I don't want it to, but it does. My eyes water, and he looks at me with concern, but I just shake my head.

"Keep going," I insist.

"You hurt," he responds.

"It's going to fucking hurt, Dagen. I get that. So fucking do it already."

He inches in a little bit further, and it's not agony, but it's not fun.

"Dag...you know the thing about the Band-Aids?" I ask him.

"What?" he asks, obviously confused.

"You can take them off fast or slow? But everyone knows it's just better to give'er?"

"You want..." He seems skeptical.

"Just go. Then stop. But like, get it in there, I can't take this slow bullshit."

And with one very quick thrust, he enters me fully. I hate myself. Why the fuck did I suggest that? It hurts so fucking badly. I look back, and Dagen is staring at me with abject pleasure, and I know he's just dying to move, but he's being patient, for me, and I fucking love him for it. He wraps a hand around my less than fully formed erection to help me forget. He leans over me.

"Jesus, sweets. The way you feel..." he murmurs. And it helps. I don't know why, exactly, but knowing that at least one of us is feeling good means something to me.

"Yeah?" I shamelessly reply, needy for praise.

"Fucking incredible."

I breathe deep and force myself to push back on him. Tell my body that this is okay, this is not a crisis. It is weird, maybe, but not bad-weird. The pain lessens to discomfort.

"Keep going," I whisper.

He remains careful, though I know he's on the very verge of losing all control.

"Fuck, Benji…you don't understand how fucking good you feel."

I reaffirm right here and now that this is not going to be a one-sided thing. As soon as I recover from this, Dag's ass is mine. He is trying to keep a rhythm going on my cock, but his hand keeps getting distracted from its tasks as he thrusts into me, trying to stay restrained. He shifts slightly, and Jesus fucking Christ yes, yes, yes, yes.

"There!" I gasp out. "Right there. Fucking hit right there again."

"Yeah? Found something you like?"

"For the love of all that is holy, do not fucking stop," I protest. "This is fucking time, not witty-quip time. Please, Dag, keep going…"

And he obliges, pace increasing inversely to depth, and I know he's close, and fuck it, so am I. I displace his hand with my own on my dick, as he's approached next to useless in that field, and start jerking myself frantically.

"Dag…" I cry out, and he hits home one last time, and I'm coming, body clenching, spilling out over my stomach. Guess it has some kind of effect on Dagen because he groans and releases, spurting off into me, and I'm breathing hard as he rabbits through his orgasm.

Finally, he pulls out, and it stings unpleasantly, but I let him pull me against him as we collapse. One wet, panting mass of breathing, sweat-slicked skin.

I never want to move again. I feel his lips on mine for a second. I murmur some sort of response. And we sleep.

Chapter Fifteen

T HINGS DON'T SEEM quite as pleasant when I wake up. We are a mess of greasy lube and crusting semen and twisted sheets. I squirm out of Dagen's grip. Or I try. Moving hurts. Everything hurts.

"Jesus, fuck," I mutter.

Dag grunts questioningly from somewhere over/under/ around me. "Hmm?"

"I fucking hurt. You and your goddamn submarine cock."

"I'm flattered, Benji, but a submarine?" Dag's voice is irritatingly gruff and sexy from sleep. "A torpedo would have been sufficient."

"I hate you."

"I'll get you some ibuprofen." Rearranging his limbs and unsticking our skin, he hops off the bed in a disgusting display of energy.

"I love you," I recant.

I flick on the bedside lamp to survey the damage. I refuse to try and fall back asleep in this mess. I grumble my way off the mattress, but my ankles gets tangled in the sheets, and I trip inelegantly, body jerking painfully as I try only semi-successfully to regain my balance. Of course ,Dagen returns just then, with the painkillers and a glass of water and a smug-ass grin.

"Shower?" he offers.

I pout. "Easy for you to say. I don't want to stand. I don't want to sit. I don't want to move. Everything is awful and it's all your fault. "

"It'll get better after the next few times," he promises, handing off the pills and kissing my shoulder.

"What makes you think there will be a next time, Dagen Mercutio?" I growl, gulping down a mouthful of ibuprofen and water.

Dagen looks temporarily panicked—one of my favourite ways for him to look, as it happens so rarely. Unfortunately, his flustered state causes me to smile, and he catches on that I'm lying a bit, and that maybe in a few days, when I forget this feeling, I might be convinced to try it again. I watch him watching me, a half-smile on his face, and I feel seen and important and stupid in love.

"C'mon," he coaxes. "Shower with me. You know we need to. And then I'll wrap you in a quilt and change the sheets and everything."

I let him lead me, groaning, into the bathroom where he proceeds to push me under the hot water and wash me all tenderly and stuff. It's weird, but nice. Really nice. He stands beside me under the spray. I lean into his chest. He wraps his arms around me. Nuzzles my ear.

"No sex, Dagen."

I feel his mouth grin into the shell of my ear.

"Worth a try," he says, and I *hmmph* my disagreement.

In a while, he stops the shower. Towels me off, wraps me in my duvet. Changes the sheets and everything.

***

"So, Lil, how's riding the third wave?" I ask, smearing a fry in vinegar. She'd phoned me earlier saying she was having a shitty day, and fried potatoes were the *only* thing that would help. That and the pleasure of my company—which was a distant second, just so I knew.

"First of all, feminism is not a joke, and second of all, I'm not a third-wave feminist, I'm an intersectional feminist. And other than assholes like you, and the other constant slew of indignities myself and other women of colour have to deal with, it's going just fine, thank you."

I open my mouth to say something along the lines of, "Christ, relax," but before I get a chance, her eyes flash with an anger I haven't seen in a long time.

"Seriously, Benj. This stuff isn't a joke to me."

I nod, like, *oh yeah, of course, I know*, but the truth is, I don't, not really.

"Right. No, you're right, I'm sorry. Something happen?"

Lillian sighs. "That was just kind of a cherry on top of a rather shitty week. Sorry for biting your head off. I mean, I'm not sorry, because I don't have to be sorry, but I know you didn't mean any harm."

"How's school?" I offer, in the world's least smooth segue.

"Ehhhhh," she replies, allowing the previous moment to pass. Her nose wrinkles adorably, and I remember, yet again, what made her so easy to love. "It's not the best. Too many labs, too many fiddly details. Not the worst, though."

"Ew," I reply, sympathetically.

She laughs. "Yeah, biology, fairly gross."

"So, you get to work with cadavers and all that?"

"Benjamin. I'm a freshman. Not med student."

"Right," I say, feeling stupid. What do I know about college anyway? "So, like, dissecting rats and frogs and stuff?"

"More like looking at slides under a microscope," she explains.

I cock my head, trying to come up with something intelligent to say, but I'm drawing a blank.

"Jesus, Benjamin, is that *another* hickey? Are you sure you're not dating a thirteen-year-old?"

"Shut up," is my brilliant comeback.

"So things are—"

"We fucked," I say, "if that's what you're getting at.

"Obviously it is." She grins. "Well?"

"What?"

"The sex. How was it?"

"We're not honestly talking about this?" I wonder aloud.

"If you can't talk about it, you shouldn't be doing it, Benjamin..." Lillian says, adopting a fake teacher voice.

"Shut up," I counter, "I *can* talk about it. I just choose not to."

"At least tell me if it was any good," she insists.

"Excuse me?"

"Well, was it?"

"Yes! Okay? Yes! It was fine. Good even. Great even!" I expound, maybe a bit too loudly.

"Well, good," she replies, and she sounds amused. I blush a little.

"Yep, sure is." I try to keep my voice more hushed this time around.

"Did it hurt?"

"Jesus Christ, Lillian, you are not serious? What makes you think I was even—"

"Well, were you?"

"Goddammit, yes, okay? Yes. I was, and it hurt, but then it felt good but still kind of hurt, and then it was over."

"Cool."

"Is it?"

"You had fun?" she asks, and I think about it, and yeah, yeah. I did have fun.

"Yeah," I reply.

"Then it's really cool. I'm happy for you, Ben, seriously. I know it's weird, but I mean it. I want you to have positive sexual experiences with people you care about."

I roll my eyes. "Sometimes you are too much, you know that? Like, a guy can only handle so much sincerity in one day, y'know?"

Lillian laughs. "Yeah, alright. Just one more bit, alright?"

"Oh, God," I reply, unenthused. "What now?"

"It's not a big deal, because I'm looking for it and stuff, but, if you want to keep this all a secret, I kind of wonder if you should be more careful?"

"More careful of what? We got tested, we're good." I insist, opting not to divulge the issue of the gonorrhoea.

"Not about that. Well, I mean, about that, too, but more about, like, media stuff. The hickeys, I mean. Like, you said there might be pictures of you and me in the park that day before Christmas, remember? And you weren't wrong. I checked some gossip sites, and there are definitely rumours circulating. I mean, I'll be your beard if you really want me to be, but I doubt that is how you want to play it, you know? Like, I can't imagine you'd like doing that to yourself. I'm not saying you need to come out, but just how deep in the closet do you want to be?"

"I'm not that worried, Lillian, like, there's Doug and Luce and I, and then there's Dagen. He's the celebrity, the rest of us are just kind of there, right? The tabloids are only going to sink their teeth into gossip about him. They're not going to lose it over what may or may not be a hickey on some nobody's neck."

"It's not just the press I'm worried about," Lillian admits. "Honestly, they aren't even the main thing. I'm just amped up about Dagen."

"What are you talking about?"

"Same thing I talked about before. When he finds out that you're seeing this mysterious guy, he's going to freak! I told you. When it comes to you, he is innately jealous."

I sigh. I guess this isn't going away.

"Lil...can we go outside, or something? I guess there is something I should tell you."

Her eyes darken slightly. I never give her enough credit.

"No," she says. And she doesn't mean *no we can't go outside because I adore these uncomfortable, plastic booths.* I think she means more along the lines of *no, oh, no, you fucking well are not,* but I need to know for sure.

"What?" I try.

"No," she repeats. "You are not. Please, Ben, please do not tell me that you are screwing *Dagen Fucking Brown*."

"So what if I am."

Her eyes glint in a way that has nothing to do with the harsh fluorescents.

"Benjamin," she says, voice flat and firm as an oak table.

"What?" I reply, like I don't know exactly what she is saying, even if she hasn't said it yet.

"Christ, seriously, Ben, what the actual fuck are you doing? Dagen? Honestly? You're saying you *honestly* don't remember what going to school with Dagen was like?"

"What do you mean, what is was like?" I bristle. "It was school. With Dagen. He was my best friend, we had fucking fun."

"Fine, he was your best friend. And that's fine. Be best friends away. But, God, Ben, what the hell are you thinking? Like, you're best friends, so you know even better than I do how much of an asshole he is. You were there, Benj. You and me watched every single fucking girl in our whole fucking grade fall for him. Every damn girl. Since like….eighth grade. You have to remember? How he'd lead them on, take them out, fuck them, and ditch them. He's such a goddamn stereotype."

I force myself to laugh and shake my head. "He won't do that to me."

"Oh, really?" Lillian's voice is dead serious.

"Really," I insist. "Fuck, Lillian. I trust him, okay? I'm in love with him."

"And you think they weren't? For God's sakes, Ben, can't you see what a good prize you'd make? The one person it would be hardest for him to get to love him, who's always seen past and weeded through his sundry bullshit? The one person who has ever had any kind of power over him? Christ, how great will it be for him to bring you down, if only to prove to himself that he can? It's his game. It's what he does. Honestly, I don't even know if he can help himself."

"He won't do that to me," I maintain, but now my traitor heart is doubting, because haven't I been telling myself this same noise this whole time? And here's Lillian, spouting off my fears, and by voicing them she's making them somehow real. But no, this fucking can't. This can't be just some game of his. It *can't*. He loves me. He does.

"How do you know? Please, Ben. Think about it." Lillian's volume is low, but her intensity is high, and her tone is so full of worry and care that I can barely cope.

"You think I haven't? You think that I haven't been obsessed with that very thought every fucking second of this relationship? I'm terrified of him not being as level as he seems."

"He isn't! Everyone knows that! Dagen couldn't be sincere if he tried!"

"You don't know him like I do!" I practically yell, and I know every bit how pathetic and desperate I sound, and add to that the fact that I'm sure we'll get kicked out of the fucking restaurant at any moment. I don't care, though. I'm fucking done. I need to get away from Lillian. I scramble up and walk—okay, speed walk—the fuck out of there.

Fuck, fuck, fuck, fuck, fuck, fuck, fuck. Jesus Christ, how could she say that shit to me? Why couldn't she just support me for this one thing, this one stupid thing that I need her for. Goddammit!

I'm out of the restaurant and I'm sprinting now. I hear her calling after me, but I don't fucking care. I just need to get away from her, from here. Get home.

***

And I do. Through the parking lot, along the strip mall, past the turnoff to the residential section, down the road, up the hill, through my parking lot. Up the stairs.

Trembling with angst, I fumble the key in the lock before finally making it fit, and fling open the apartment door. And he's there. Dagen's not on the phone with the tabloids admitting everything, or laughing it up with a cool new friend. He hasn't packed up all his shit and left just to hurt me. He's just sitting there. Playing the fucking Wii.

And he grins at me. Like he's so fucking happy to see me. He says, "Hey, sugar, what's shaking?" or something dumb like that, and I practically fucking leap on him because I was right and she was wrong.

"Do you love me?" I ask, and it's almost a whimper, my lips at his ear, body flush against his.

He quirks an eyebrow at me. "Of course I do."

And that is all I need.

Almost drunk with adrenaline, I pull him off the couch, into the bedroom, stripping us down as fast as I can, needing the contact, the realness that flesh on flesh provides.

"Whoa, Benji, what's up, did something happen?" I hear him ask, but I don't answer, kneading instead at his chest while my tongue overpowers his in his mouth.

Barely remembering to grab the lube, I hike his hips upwards, looming over him. Despite my unexpected need, he's hard beneath me, and I'm glad. I rock my hips, grating us against each other, making him whimper.

I pour the stuff into my hand, and it leaks onto the carpet, but I can't bring myself to care. I quickly coat my finger, and reach between us, finding his asshole with my finger and penetrating him roughly, feeling vaguely guilty for not being gentle with him like he was with me. I kiss him harder to try and make up for it, pulsing my finger in and out of him. I add another finger faster than I should.

"Fuck, Benji, what—"

I don't let him get any more words in, so afraid he'll ask me to stop. I keep kissing him, stretching the ring impatiently. He kisses me back hard and opens his legs wider, arching his back to press into me.

Suddenly, it all seems wrong to me. I don't know what. Something about the way we're lying, or... It reminds me too much of Lillian.

I pull out my fingers, and grunt something about wanting to fuck him from behind. He rolls over, and I straddle his calves, pulling back at his hips. Our mouths no longer touch, but he doesn't try to speak. I scramble for more lube before shoving my fingers inside him again, sucking on his shoulder blade. I reach under him, and find his cock. It is solid and warm and reassuring in my hand.

He moans encouragingly and then grunts as I add another finger.

"Benj..." he says softly.

"Please," I whisper.

"Do it," he demands.

I pull out and use my thumb to stretch his ass cheek over, exposing the small gape of his ass, and I want him. I want him rough, and my own intensity freaks me out. I'm afraid I'll hurt him, that he'll cry out or stop me, but he doesn't, he just presses back against me.

"Fuck me," he insists.

I align my cock with the rim of his asshole. He's tight and unyielding, and his breath hitches below me, but he doesn't flinch. The head of my cock pries him open, and I almost can't believe that it fits. The glorious grip of his ass on me is overwhelmingly perfect. I grip his shoulder with one hand and force myself deeper, grunting with effort and the pleasure, and his greedy ass swallows my cock.

I jerk him faster, relieved that his erection hasn't evaporated, but it's hard to concentrate because the tight ring of muscle gripping the base of my cock is so incredible. I drag back and feel that pressure course along the length of my cock. I try not to move again, try to give him time to adjust, but I'm too needy to be generous. I give an experimental thrust, and when he doesn't complain, I do it again and then again, until I can't stop between them because I'm already so close and he feels so hot and tight and I never want to not be allowed to do this.

And it must be alright enough, because Dag's now riding the rhythm, pushing back to meet me when I shove forward over him. I cling to his shoulder, wanting him impossibly closer. Everything's been so fast, but there's just so much inside of me that I can't hold on, I really can't, and I sink my teeth into his shoulder blade. I scream as he moans, and we come and we come and we come, and we are all at once and together, and all I can feel is relief as I fold over him, exhausted in a way I've never been before.

I lie beside Dagen, let him hold me to his chest, feel his breath in my hair. In return, he allows the silence between us to stretch for hours.

"So," he says, finally, after we've slept and awoken, my breath and body steadied. "Are you going to tell me what that was about?"

I turn and kiss him. "Shower first?" I wheedle.

"Fine," he agrees.

He follows me into the en suite. I flick on the bathroom stereo, and Antony and the Johnsons send slow echoes in among the tiles. Dagen turns on the water. He stands with his eyes closed, the water hot, streaming down his body, his undoubtedly sore muscles relaxing under its weight.

"I didn't mean to hurt you," I whisper. He smiles slightly and opens his eyes.

"No damage done, Benji. Opposite of damage, actually." He ropes me in towards him, an arm around my back. For a long second, he looks into my eyes and then kisses me slowly, testing, his eyes pointedly open, studying my face.

I close my eyes. Sink into the kiss, my guilt and fear finally draining from me. His mouth moves against mine, calming and sure. I keep kissing him, arms slipping around his neck, and I don't care if I'm needy, because he lets me be, he soothes the want. At last we fade apart, and I drop my head onto his shoulder while he palms slow circles into my back.

We wash each other carefully, curiously, exploring each other without the lust that usually comes with being naked. I kiss his shoulder, and he kisses my cheek.

We dry and dress. He pulls on a pink t-shirt because he can, and he asks me if I want anything to eat.

I don't. It's evening now, the sky a monotonous grey outside the window.

He sits on the couch patiently. I shuffle around awkwardly for a bit.

"Benji," he says after a few moments. And I sit. Close.

I trace the lines and veins on his hand with my fingertips.

"I went out with Lillian today," I start, even though I know he knows, because I told him where I was going when I left the house this afternoon. "And...she just said some shit that kind of freaked me out."

"About me." It isn't a question.

"Yeah."

"Like?"

"Just typical bullshit about how I shouldn't trust you because you'll only end up hurting me. Which I've been trying to tell myself isn't true since we started this thing. And I'd finally started believing myself, so I freaked. And I shouldn't have. And I know we aren't really telling anyone, so I'm sorry, but she's been a really good friend to me up until now...and—"

"Are you okay now?" he interrupts me, fingers tightening around mine.

"Yeah."

"Okay. That's what matters, alright?"

I nod, letting this final layer of relief carry me down. I wriggle out from his hold and stretch out over the couch to rest my head on his leg, and he runs his fingers through my hair like I was hoping he would.

"Are *you* okay?" I ask.

"Yeah, for the most part," he replies. "Kinda pissed, but I guess I shouldn't have expected anything different from her."

"Why do you guys hate each other so much, anyway?" I ask lazily.

"I don't know." He shrugs. Not admitting it has anything to do with me, not like Lillian keeps pressing.

"Dag?" I ask, after a while.

"Mm?"

"How long...have you felt this? About me? Like, you know. Like this."

"I don't know," he answers. "A while."

I can tell he's not exactly telling the truth, but it's like he just doesn't want to, and I guess it's not that important, so I let it slide. I figure he'll tell me eventually.

We lapse into silence, and I close my eyes, feeling his fingers brush my scalp. After a while, I turn over so I'm looking upwards into his face. He smiles, leans down and kisses me, but there's a sort of uncertainty in his eyes that scares me a bit, like we're slowly cultivating a distance.

I wish that instead of all those I don't knows, there had been truths instead.

"You sure I didn't hurt you?" I ask, needing to change the subject, and the cockiness rushes back into his expression.

"Sugar," he asserts, "you couldn't hurt me if you tried." He grins, and I smack him, and he kisses me. I squirm, and he pins me. And we make out.

Chapter Sixteen

L ILLIAN AND I make up eventually. Or sort of. She apologizes and says she's got my back and will shut her mouth about Dagen. She goes on about how all she wants is for me to be happy and it wasn't her place, and how she would hate it if I said anything like that to her. She's sincere so far as I can tell; she cries a bit, and we hug and go for a walk.

Dagen doesn't understand why I've forgiven her, but I tell him to leave it alone.

Today, though, today I'm anxious, because it is my goddamn birthday and they will both be there. They goddamn better behave themselves or I swear, I will become violent.

I'm just having a kind of get-together, nothing big, just Luce, Doug, Abby, Dag, Lils and Radley—who I will be meeting for the first time—and maybe a couple of girls if Luce and Doug feel like bringing dates.

We told them. Dag and I, I mean. And I don't know what it is about this city that makes everyone so complacent. Lucifer practically killed himself laughing, fell off his drum stool and cackled on the floor, and now makes very lame gay jokes whenever possible. Doug just nodded seriously and that was it. It's like he knew it was coming. Though, considering Doug, I'm not surprised.

Maybe it's the whole silence thing, but the guy's got an aura of wisdom to him. It's unmistakable. So he probably did know it was coming. Luce still shakes his head and goes on about how he can't believe it, and how he'd "take cunt over asshole any day."

159

It is annoying as fuck, but then, Lucifer is annoying as fuck, so no real surprise there. I'm mostly just glad there's no sneaking around or secrets between us prior to us starting to record our album next month.

So tonight, we're grabbing dinner out, then heading back to my place for drinks. Lots of drinks, I'm guessing. I just want to get wasted and be stupid and maybe end the night with some sloppy sex with Dagen.

Dag and I arrive first. It's only my twentieth, but we don't get ID'd, so he buys me a drink. Nice microbrew, and it tastes really good, probably just because it's my birthday, and my friends are going to show up. I had lunch with my parents, and Dagen's squeezing my thigh under the table; everything just seems to kind of work right now. So I'm smiling, and Dag smirks at me amusedly and says I look goofy, but then he's smiling, too.

"Hey."

I look up. Lillian is standing nervously next to me, trying to avoid even sort of facing Dagen. Standing next to her, there is a broad-shouldered tall guy with glasses and a Seahawks cap.

"Hey!" I say, genuinely happy. I stand up and shake Radley's hand, and he seems like a decent guy, at least, from his vibe, which is great, because Lillian deserves someone decent. There's the standard shuffling off of coats and scraping of chairs until they've sat themselves down, Lillian across from me and Radley across from Dagen.

Radley introduces himself, and Dagen makes some comment on the Seahawks, and they do the sports small talk thing for a bit while Lillian asks about my lunch with my folks. It is surprisingly not awful and remains that way until Doug, Abby, and Luce show up.

"Hey, guys!" I'm relieved to see them, because Dagen knows even less about football than I do, and conversation is bound to dry up at any moment. For once, I'm happy to have Luce yammering away about the metro and chucking a gift certificate at my head.

Thankfully, Abby sits next to Lillian, and since they have kind of become friends over the years, they pick up a conversation easily enough. As a result, Lils and Dagen aren't in forced proximity to each other, and everything is alright enough. I wonder if maybe that should make me anxious, but I say fuck it and take a long sip of my draught.

"Fuck, Ben." It's Lucifer. "How the fuck are you? I haven't seen you for, like, three days. Man, the other day, I was at the skate park, and this chick comes up to me, and she totally recognizes me, and, like, is trying to get me to sign her tits or something. But she is, like, fucking thirteen, and I am like, 'Shit, man, I'll sign whatever you want, but keep your shirt on, I'm not going to fucking jail over this.'"

"Christ, Helner, I've never known you to show such foresight," Dagen remarks dryly.

Lucifer looks at him, sheepish. "Yeah, well, no one else is gonna play your drums and take your shit, man."

Dag laughs. "God, I can see you now, arms outstretched and palms pulsating with shit—"

"Fucking gross, Dagen," Abby interjects. Dagen raises his eyebrows and flashes her a grin. She tosses her head and resumes her conversation with Lillian.

"I said take your shit, not hold your shit, asshole," Luce mutters.

Doug sits silently beside Lucifer, looking amused, but then, Lucifer tends to eternally amuse Doug, whereas he just generally annoys the rest of us.

"Shut up, Lucifer," Dagen tries half-heartedly.

"Benj, have you heard the new Bolted album?" Luce asks me.

"Oh, Christ," Dagen answers before I can reply. "Not another one of your underground start-ups. I, stupidly, gave you the benefit of the doubt and checked out their profile, and surprise, surprise, they are fucking screamo posers devoid of talent."

"Are not!" Luce argues. "They've got a kind of Taking Back Sunday vibe going on, and I'm really digging them—"

"No. No, fuck you. No way. TBS at least offers some interesting harmonies and actual lyrics. Bolted is just banal screamo. I'm not against harder shit, but if you're screaming to muffle your weak-ass lyrics, we've got a problem."

"Okay, maybe not TBS. Maybe more like Dashboardthing..." Lucifer tries.

"Dude," Dagen says, voice ripe with disdain, "for fuck's sakes, stop talking. You're embarrassing yourself. Bolted is a screamo band. They sound like a fucking screamo band. Get a fucking clue."

Lucifer sulks and sucks on the straw of his rum and Coke. Luckily, or more like unluckily, for us, he will rebound in about 2.3 seconds.

***

After dinner, we head out to our cars. Doug has parked next to Dag, and he hands me a case of beer. No one would ever dream of ID-ing Doug. If anyone even considered asking, they'd get that impeccably condescending look, one of complete disgust, and the clerk would immediately swallow their words. It's something I like to see now and then, people quaking with the fear of Doug.

He's standing at the passenger side so he closes the door behind Luce and nods. We assume that means he'll meet us there. Luce is drumming on the dash.

Lillian and Radley climb into his Chevy Silverado, and she says she'll follow us because she hasn't been to my apartment before. Probably because Dagen is basically always there.

"So?" I ask inside the car. "Will you survive the night?"

"Mm," Dagen agrees. "It wasn't so bad."

"Told you she'd be good."

"Told you I'd be good."

I kiss him. He kisses me back. I was going for quick, but he doesn't stop. He knows Lillian is watching us, waiting for us to pull out so she and Radley can follow. He's being a possessive little bastard, which is stupid, because Lillian is obviously happy with the new guy, and I am obviously happy with Dagen, but I figure I'll let him indulge for a little while. I'm buzzed enough to not complain. He's got his hand cupping the back of my neck, and the yearning little noises he's making are enough to make my dick twitch—a fact that isn't helped by him dragging his fingers up my inner thigh. I'm less inhibited than normal, and I hear myself moan appreciatively. The party. Right. Fuck.

"Dag…" I try.

"Ben…" he mimics. His hand is drawing too close to my crotch, and I shove it away.

"Dagen," I say more firmly, trying to break off the kiss. He just presses me into the window.

"C'mon, sweetness…let me…bet I can make you come in two minutes."

"I bet you couldn't, because I'm not fucking going to get off with my ex-wife watching," I say, giving him enough of a shove to show him I'm serious.

He pouts and mutters, "Spoilsport," before finally removing himself and starting the car.

"Benji?" he asks, as he reverses out of the parking space.

"Yeah?"

"I love you."

He looks very serious. Not bad serious. Just trying very hard to make sure I get this. That I know this is true.

"I love you, too," I reply, giving him an odd little look for his odd little assertion.

He kisses me quickly as he shifts into drive.

***

We get back to my apartment, Lillian and Radley right behind us.

"Just wait a sec," Dagen mutters as I go to open the car door.

"What?"

"Well, there's going to be people and stuff, but I got you something. I just can't give it to you."

I raise my eyebrows suggestively.

"Oh, really?"

"Not sex."

"Disappointed! Why can't you give it to me, then?"

"I don't know. I just don't want to in front of everyone, that's all awkward. And it's kind of lame."

"Okay..."

"So, it's in our sock drawer. But you have to wait until everyone else goes home. I just didn't want you to think that I didn't get you anything, or something."

He's being kind of jittery, which is fairly abnormal for Dag. He moves to open the door.

"Dag." He looks at me. "Thanks."

"You haven't seen it yet."

"I don't care. Thanks."

And I almost want to go upstairs and tell everyone to get the hell out and fuck that nervous smile off Dag's mouth. But that would be rude. And I'd regret it later. Everyone will leave eventually and I'll get him all to myself at some time tonight. So it's fine.

I grab his arm and pull him in to kiss him. Sometimes I wonder if I'll ever get over the feeling of his lips on mine.

No, I decide. I definitely won't.

***

It's a good party, or get-together or whatever. I'm drunk—not sloppy drunk, but definitely beyond buzzed, and just kind of friendly and chatty and maybe a bit cuddly. From the glare that Dagen sends anyone I get too close to, I'm definitely too cuddly. And it's that look that is probably inspiring me to be more so. So, I'm a bad person. I just like making him get that flash of jealousy. He's fucking possessive and needs to chill, so really, I'm just demonstrating that. Abby pats my cheek when I tell her she has pretty hair, and even Doug lets me sit on the arm of the couch next to him and press my forehead into his shoulder and tell him just how much I like the beer he got me.

Radley left…at some point? Said he had to work early. I'm fairly certain Lucifer is very, very drunk. Maybe even more drunk than me. He's rifling through my shit and putting on a new CD every three seconds. Doug's expression is…mellow. He's so weird. He just sits and watches us most of the time. Abby went home after the restaurant; her boyfriend got off work and she was going to meet him. So it's just us four and Lillian, who is also apparently in an alcohol-induced chill.

What I like about drinking is that once you're buzzed, you don't really have to be doing anything. You can float around a room and kind of babble or watch music videos, and everything is just so much fun. Basically, I'm doing nothing. But I'm having a very, very good time.

But getting tired. I guess I was sort of tired to begin with, and alcohol always makes me more tired. Dagen is sitting on the couch, so I think I will go burrow into him. Fuck who's watching. I want to be kissed.

"Luce, put on a movie," I direct and then forget to watch what he picks. Knowing Luce, it will have plenty of explosions. I use the time while Luce is fiddling around with the DVD remote to sidle under Dagen's arm, encouraging him to wrap it around me. It doesn't take too much effort, once he realizes what I want. Lillian is quasi-napping on the La-Z-Boy.

I'm falling asleep fast on Dagen's chest while Luce talks at the TV, arguing with the characters. He might be high on something. Not positive. Don't particularly care. I notice vaguely that Dagen isn't even slightly drunk, which I seem to think is unusual. I try to ask him about it, but the idea gets a little garbled from my brain to my mouth so I give up on it, pressing my ear into his shoulder. He's got his fingers rubbing my arm aimlessly while I alternate between watching the movie and Lucifer and closing my eyes and just being.

I remember my original intention and nuzzle up to Dagen, trying to get him to kiss me. He does, but only once, and it's short.

"Not now, sugar. People are around, and if we start, I doubt I'll stop. You don't wanna give everyone a show."

"I won't, I promise!" I whine, but he won't give. I stretch out with him behind me instead. His hand slips over my abs, and I figure it's all I need so I prepare to drift off.

It's been a half hour or so, I'm guessing, but Luce is nudging me awake. Doug and Luce have called a cab and it's arrived. I give them both a drunken hug. Lucifer is wasted, and Doug patiently helps him feed his hands into the arm holes of his coat.

I want to collapse back into Dagen again, but when I try, he walks me to my bedroom—our bedroom—and pushes me onto the bed. He kisses me. Helps me take off my socks and jeans. Covers me in quilt. Kisses me again. And I'm out.

***

"I'm glad you're awake."

I wake up. But the voice isn't talking to me. It's Lillian, my mind clarifies, and I'm almost completely sober now. I look at the clock. 4:07 a.m. Weird time to be awake.

"Yeah." I hear Dagen's voice, thick with sleep like I've heard it a thousand times. I sit up, thinking I need a piss and some water, and then maybe I'll join them.

Before I can do anything, though, I hear Lillian saying, "We need to talk about this." She's using her *you've been a bad boyfriend but I'm going to be mature and we'll talk to out, by which I mean I'll lecture you* voice, which I've also heard a thousand times, and I never want to be in the same room as it again. I feel like I'm dropping the through line. Talk about what? To who?

"What's there to talk about?" Dagen's voice has a sharp edge to it that he never uses with me. *Leave whatever the hell it is alone, Lillian*, I want to say. That voice never leads anywhere good. The person on the receiving end usually ends up in tears.

"You know what."

I don't know what. And I don't understand why he knows what.

"Fine. What needs to be said?" Dagen's terseness is mounting.

"You didn't tell him?" Lillian's voice is quiet, but the door is open, and the apartment is too fucking small. I know I don't want to hear this, but it's too fucking late now.

"I didn't tell him," Dagen confirms.

"I didn't, either."

"Good. No point. I don't want to put him through that," Dagen says, in a discussion-closed kind of way. But Lillian doesn't ever let someone else close a discussion.

"Yeah."

Dagen exhales with what sounds like frustration, and I can just picture the look she's probably giving him. The "don't you even *think* we're done here, Benjamin" look. Except that he's not me. But he might as well be. I know what causes someone to sigh like that.

"Is that all, Paresky, 'cause I'd really like to go to bed. You know? With my boyfriend?"

"Tell me you won't hurt him." Her voice is low, urgent, almost pleading. I want to roll my eyes and dismiss this whole thing as

Lillian being overprotective, but "tell me what" is on repeat in my brain.

"I'm not the one who cheated on him."

My insides turn as cold as Dagen's tone of voice. I'm not still in love with her, so I guess, technically, it shouldn't matter. But she never told me. Here I am, trying so hard to hold on to some semblance of a relationship. Goddammit. I don't know what to feel. Angry or hurt or sad or…I just feel empty. I think I want to cry. No. I don't want to care. I want to piss and have some water and forget I ever heard any of this. It's over. Dagen's with me now, and Lillian and I were over a hundred years ago and—

"You as good as cheated on him. It takes two to create an unwanted pregnancy, Dagen." Her voice is biting, and I'm uncomprehending, or rejecting, because *what the fuck is she talking about*? "Goddammit, Dagen, you came this close to ruining my life, and I won't let you ruin his. Not this time." Her pace and tone are reaching frantic levels, but they're fucking lackadaisical in comparison to my own internal frenzy.

No.

No. Not happening. My brain pieces it together too fast, too fast, I didn't want to know this. My heart sinks into my stomach, shoving its contents upwards, and I'm stumbling for the doorway and I'm choking, and Dagen and Lillian look at me, horror written on their faces, and all I can think to say is, "Too late."

It's too late. I'm crumbling, devastated, fragmented. I'm retching into the bathroom sink because the toilet seemed just too far away, and the two of them are rushing at me, and I'm slamming the door because I won't. I won't get sucked into their banging on the door, their pleading, their "Benji!"s and "it was a long time ago"s and "let us explain"s. We're done. I'm done with him, and I'm done with her. And I'm going to tell them.

I fling open the door, and I think there might be vomit on my shirt, but I don't fucking care because this needs to be said.

"Get the fuck out of here." I'm so mad I can't even scream. My voice is so low it shakes, and my eyes are burning because I want to cry, but I don't want to cry over them, because how could they? Christ. How could they? They almost left me to raise his fucking kid, and I wouldn't have even known. Never even would have questioned.

"Benj—" Lillian tries, but I cut her off.

"I never...you... I would never have cheated on you. I was miserable, Lillian, absolutely fucking pathetically miserable with you. But I married you. And I would have stayed faithful to you my whole life it that's what it took."

"It was just one time, Ben, I swear..." she whispers, but I guess the look on my face tips her off that once or a thousand times wouldn't make a difference, and suddenly she's crying, racing down the hall, towards the front door, and most of me doesn't even care at all.

"Benji..." Dagen says, voice quiet, trying to calm me.

"*Don't fucking call me that!*" I'm shaking so bad my lungs hurt. "I trusted you. I was so scared. That you'd fuck this up. I told myself. Be careful, Benjamin, you've seen what Dagen can do and will do and on and on and on. And I blew it all off. I gave you one chance, because you were so sweet and told me such nice things and... I'm fucking stupid and pathetic to have believed a single word you've said."

He's crying. He's got fucking tears careening down his fucking perfect cheeks, and I don't care. I don't. It's just another fucking act.

"Benji, please..."

"Get out, Dagen. Get out of here. This is my place. Mine. And I will not let you pollute the only thing I have left."

"Benji, believe me, I love you I—"

"Don't. I'll be out tomorrow. Between nine-thirty and noon. Get your shit out of my apartment. And fucking slide the key under the door. I don't want to see it. I don't want to ever think of you again."

"Benji, please." His voice is a soft little whisper.

I don't fucking care. This thing here. This was a mistake.

"I told you I didn't want this to be a mistake. Now get out or I'll call the fucking cops." I finally break, and I'm fucking crying. He goes to hug me but I dart away and slam the bathroom door, locking it, and I scream, now, finally. I tell him to get the fuck away from me, because everything is over.

Chapter Seventeen

I DON'T SLEEP.

It's eight a.m. and I am still sitting in a chair, glass of water untouched in front of me. I've remembered every moment so many times I've lost count, and all it does is make me ache. I can't believe I told him to come get his stuff. Not today. But I won't be here if he comes early. I won't be that mopey, pathetic little ass-wipe that sits at home hoping to catch a glimpse of their ex.

My throat clenches. *Ex.* I never wanted to have a fucking ex ever again. I force myself to shower. Get dressed. Brush my teeth. Grab my iPod. Leave the house. Walk for hours. Making a list of things in my head, things I can't ever think about again. Music, mostly. I have to keep fucking skipping songs because they are him. Blink and MCR and Bright Eyes and TBS. All have him attached to them. And if the song isn't him then it's way too fucking close to how I'm feeling or it's way too happy, and so, I switch on some old The Used and suddenly I'm just running. Sprinting like I did before all of this, when I was sprinting towards him instead of away from him.

When my lungs feel raw and my throat bloody, I finally stop. Collapse on wet grass, feel it seeping into my skin. Maybe I'll get sick.

Finally, I stand. I wander towards Doug's house. Some silence to numb my mind. But Luce's car is parked out front, and there's not a chance I could even stand Luce for a second.

I realize that I don't want to tell anyone. I don't want anyone to know that I've been burned. Don't want any I-knew-it looks or sympathy or anything.

I don't want anything. Not anything I can have.

***

It's two p.m. He should be gone by now. I'm covered in sweat and stink of wet grass, and I just ache. I slowly head back home.

And he's gone. He's removed himself from my apartment. His shirts and movies and crappy CDs and everything. It was supposed to help, but it's like someone has evacuated my heart.

I crawl into bed. It's okay. I will allow myself this. One day of utter wallowing.

I'm crying when the phone rings. I pick it up automatically.

"Benji?" He's surprised I answered. Him and me both.

I hang up.

He phones back, but I don't pick up this time. Listen to him from my cavern of blankets.

"Benji...please, baby. I just want to talk to you. I can't do this. Please. Pick up the phone. Or call me. Please."

He hangs up.

I don't call back.

***

It's been four days.

Four fucking soul-sucking agonising post-breakup days.

It's supposed to get easier, but, of course, it doesn't. I guess I'm doing the whole grieving thing, because as of this morning, I'm angrier than hell. Him and her both constantly leave messages on my machine. I don't care. I'm trying not to care. I want to smash their faces in, in the least poetic way possible.

I've taken to singing along, very loudly, to self-indulgent emo albums.

I've unloaded my treadmill from my storage cupboard. I refuse to be anything less than productive. And I'm running and singing and gasping and crying and I'm a stupid fucking mess of a human.

Lacey sings in my ear, and I sing along to "Jude Law and a Semester Abroad," except I sub "love" for "miss," because I'm so incredibly, pathetically lame like that. Fuck him. Really. Fuck him. The song's on repeat, and really do fucking hope the next boy he kisses gives him something...for all of, like one second.

I almost trip off the fucking treadmill because a picture hits my brain, and the thought of him actually kissing literally anyone else fucking kills me. So now I've got a skinned knee and even my favourite emo anthem is doing absolutely shit for me.

"YOU RUIN EVERYTHING."

That's the nice thing about living alone. You can yell as much as you fucking want and no one gets mad at you. Well, I live in an apartment, so I guess, technically, someone could get mad at me...but I have good insulation. I hope.

But that's the only nice thing about living alone. The bad things are that it's lonely and boring, and I miss him so fucking much I want to eat my own liver.

Fuck. Goddamn. I am *not* thinking about missing him. Even if it is fucking true.

I need to fill in all this fucking time.

I go to the drug store. Dye my hair back to its fucking normal color. Brown. My hair is brown. All that fucking black hair dye was just a result of him. Just like every other fucking thing in my whole life. I wash it with the included conditioner, and I don't put in any fucking product.

I clean. Music loud in my ears, "Three Cheers for Sweet Revenge," and I'm frantically tackling every single crevice and corner, alphabetizing, scrubbing, dusting, vacuuming, polishing, and I barely even have a fucking thing worth polishing. It's spotless. It was also so damn messy with him.

And now it's just empty. I even miss his stupid mess.

I hate this. I hate how almost everything makes me feel like fucking crying. I hate crying. I hate my nose being plugged up and my cheeks going red and my brain collapsing in around depressing thought after depressing thought. I need out, but I have no idea how to get out of this.

Before, if he had hurt me, I would've talked to Lillian. I think I've always known that.

But guess I didn't think that one through.

The phone rings. It's him. I pick it up so I can hang it up without another one of his desperate messages. Leave me alone, for Christ's sake. Leave me the fuck alone.

I do my laundry. Make up a big garbage bag full of shit I don't wear anymore. Phone some charity and arrange a pick-up date. I'm a machine. I don't need anyone to help me feel efficient.

I just need someone to make me feel alive.

***

Dagen's present is sitting on my kitchen counter. I found it this morning while organizing my sock drawer because I'm a goddamn freak. It's a CD. Well, I'm assuming. It's in a clear jewel case, a piece of white paper covering the top. I don't know what to do with it.

Most of me is threatening to stick it down the garbage disposal. But that inner core part of me is pretty desperate to do otherwise.

It's just a fucking birthday present. It's been two fucking weeks. And I've proved to myself, repeatedly, that I don't need him to make me function. And so what if I haven't told anyone? I figure he can be in charge of telling Luce and Doug why we haven't had a single jam session even though we're supposedly heading to studio in just under two weeks.

I guess I should let my parents know. I made up an excuse last week for him not coming to dinner. But tomorrow night, I'm supposed to go again.

I will tell them, I decide. Verbalizing it will make it real. And it is, no matter how much I don't want it to be. I won't tell them the reason. They love him, and I don't want him to hurt them, too. I'll just say that it didn't work out.

The phone rings. I check the caller ID, and of course it's him. I don't answer. Let the machine pick it up. I'm working on becoming immune to the desperation in his voice, but it isn't working very well. I hate that not being with him makes me almost as unhappy as the betrayal. I must be some kind of a masochist.

"Hey," his voice echoes onto the machine. "It's me. Don't...give up on me, Benji. I know I deserve it...but don't. I love you, okay? And I'm sorrier than you'll ever know. Just...call me. Please."

His tone has shifted to defeat, and it almost breaks my heart all over again. But I'm so angry. So incredibly enraged that he can have effect after effect on me. Why the fuck should I feel badly for him? I'm the one who got fucked over here. I hurl the jewel case at the wall.

My intention was to shatter its innards and send a shiny, splintered rainbow into the air. Of course, physics doesn't work like that, so instead, I dent the wall with a corner, break the plastic, and a CD and a little slip of paper fall rather gracelessly to the floor.

And there he is, messing up my apartment all over again.

I crouch to clean it up.

Of course the paper has to be face up. Black ink. Messy Dagen-scrawl.

Benji–
We're emo, so here ya go, I made you a mix tape.
In CD form. But whatever, I love you.
Dagen.

And that's it. Nothing revolutionary. No "P.S. There is a deep dark secret we need to discuss and I'm begging you to keep me even after I tell you." It is still mockingly obvious that he had no intentions of ever telling me.

Unfortunately, it seems to put me into a fucking moment of weakness, because against my screaming and berating better judgment, I put the fucking thing into the stereo.

It's from Dagen so of course it starts up with some Blink. "I Miss You." And, *of course*, I can remember when he heard it first, bought the album the fucking day it came out.

And the memory smothers me.

"Listen to this, Benji." We were on my couch, him sticking an earbud in my ear. Before I ever knew he wanted me, before I knew the texture of his mouth.

"It's about you, because you're already Jiminy fucking Cricket." He grinned, and I shoved him off the couch. His fucking voice of reason, as he'd decided the night before, as I begged him off that one last shot of tequila which I knew would send him over into puke territory. As I tucked condoms in his pockets as he headed towards hotel rooms with strangers.

I press the skip button after the first chorus. I don't want to think about it. It follows with one of our songs. The one in which we alluded to "I Miss You."

> *...And if you're the voice inside my head*
> *can't you read what I have said*
> *decode our stupid moments, not the metaphorical*
> *kind*
> *Just...never mind.*

I skip it, because it's sort of becoming clear to me and I don't want it to. Goddammit.

A fast one. Another by us, which is kind of weird, because I don't tend to make a habit of listening to my own band, for fuck's sakes. Dagen's mocking falsetto looping over itself in his standard chaos.

And honey did I mention
How close you're kind of getting
and maybe you don't know it
but you're fucking leading me on
or is it me that's close to you
and what are you going to do...can't tell you how I
love that you do absolutely nothing

The internet gossip had dubbed the song "too rapey." But I'm suddenly getting that it was more than Dagen fucking around and being scandalous. I skip it. But it's a bit too late because I can feel his hand on my hip, breath hitting my neck, girls screaming in the crowd.

It goes on. "Lua" plays. I skip it.

Another song. Another fucking memory. Or not so subtle hint. Until...

The last song. I haven't heard it before. It's just him. Based around a Taking Back Sunday line, except it's skewed. Because it's Dagen.

Because I'm writing every song about you.

It's a little fucking acoustic number, and I can't even listen to the rest of the lyrics, but I still find myself putting it on repeat. And curling on the floor. And pretending not to cry.

My phone rings.

It's him.

I answer.

"They're all about me." My voice is hoarse and low, and I can hear him swallow because everything seems suddenly hyper-sensitized.

"What?" he practically gasps.

"The songs, Dagen. Goddammit. Practically all the songs you've ever written allude to *me*."

"I told you. When I named the band. You wouldn't get it—even if I told it to you."

"I thought you were kidding."

"I wasn't."

"How long?"

He's quiet. I know he knows what I mean, but he won't answer.

"Goddammit, Dagen, just tell me. How long have you…"

"Loved you?"

"Yeah. Whatever."

"Years."

"Oh." My eyes relinquish a few more droplets, and I swipe at my nose.

"Benji…" His voice is low, pleading. "Can I come over?"

I breathe. "Fine."

I hang up. Shower. Try to stop my eyes from looking so goddamn red.

Chapter Eighteen

H E KNOCKS, EVEN though I know he kept a key, I guess to be polite. I momentarily consider not answering. Afraid of what will happen if I open the door and let all this come flooding back in. But I know I can't do that. Need to face him. This. Whatever.

He's standing, obviously just-showered, like me, hands thrust deep into the pockets of what I'm pretty sure is my black zip-up. And goddamn, it's awkward. He shuffles his feet and I fidget with the doorknob.

"Hey," I venture.

He looks up, catching my eyes for just a second, but then, it's like the motion startles him, so he looks back at his sneakers again.

"Hi," he answers.

I kind of freeze. Forget what to do.

"Can I...come in?" He sounds so uncertain, and it's fucking weird. This is Dagen. Uncertain isn't in Dagen's range of emotions.

"Uh, yeah." I move half out of the way and he steps past me, his body entering my personal sphere for just a moment, not-so-gently reminding me of what we can have. That secret buzzing energy between us.

"You dyed your hair," he offers.

"Uh, yeah." I tug at my bangs a little.

"Looks good." He's quiet. Eyes studying my face.

We're still standing transitionally near the front entrance, neither of us apparently sure whether or not he's staying or going.

But he's here in front of me again. Waiting for me. It's too much to process. I slump back, letting my head tap the drywall.

"Can I kiss you?" His words come out in a nervous rush, a repeat of me and Lillian, sixteen and beside a bench, just reversed now, me being asked instead of doing the asking, me being overwhelmed with alighted nerves, and not fears of rejection.

"What?" I don't know what else to say. "No!" Except I want... "Yes. I don't know."

He gnaws uncertainly on his lip for a confused moment. But then he kisses me, lips swift against mine, like it's the only thing in all of this he's sure about. His hand, fingers curled into his palm, resting on my cheek. Fleeting 'til I turn my head. Because I should. Because there are things to be said.

"Thank you," he whispers, and I walk down the hall, into the kitchen. Fill two glasses with water to distract us from what we have to do.

We sip slowly and in unison, our eyes meeting over the spotless kitchen table.

"You know I need to know why," I say, finally.

He shakes his head. Not at me, more to himself. "I lied."

I almost smirk. "You don't say."

"No, a different time."

Cold streaks down my body, but I don't speak.

"I said before I didn't work at it. You know. When we...started. I said that I didn't try to make people feel like they were the only one. Or whatever. But...I do. Well, I did."

"So..."

"So, I worked at it. I was mad, Benji. I was mad that you had chosen her over me. And it was so wrong of me. I know it. And I'm sorry in all the ways I know how to be, but...it's the only thing I was ever good at. Reading people. Figuring them out and getting under their skin. All I wanted was for her to break everything off with you."

"So you…?"

"It was at a party. You know, one of those parties you hated, where everyone is acting like teenagers because they are teenagers and you never really quite got that, and you pleaded sick and went home early. Things were shit between you two already…and she was just telling me about it. Because she was a bit drunk, and I was pretending to be. She was mad about something stupid, like how you didn't pay her enough attention in front of other people, because she never got that you're just not that kind of a guy.

"And it was so easy, Benji, so fucking easy, because all she wanted was attention, and I knew how to give that to her. And I was so surprised, so surprised, because she was so off-limits. I didn't think it would happen, and then it was too late and I realized it could happen, that I have that kind of control. I was so mad. So fucking mad, Benji, because how could I have that over her? Over anyone? How come I could get absolutely everyone to love me except for the one person that I actually fucking loved? Love. That I actually fucking *love*."

He's crying and I wish he wouldn't, because he's Dagen and he doesn't cry, but he is anyway. I can't stand it, because the story doesn't make anything any better. He's still just so fucking hard not to forgive.

"That's a shit excuse, Dagen!" And *I'm* mad. I'm angry. Why couldn't he have told me that she seduced him. That she was to blame, that it was a horrible accident, that she was wearing a mask, and it was a total mistake and unavoidable, could've happened to anyone, not this stupid, fucking truth. Because I want him. I want him so badly I can't remember to think, to see, to breathe. "Why'd you have to go and fucking tell me that?"

He looks surprised. I guess he should be, too. He was expecting hurt, and I am, but not just that. I'm something more.

"Why would you tell me that, Dagen?" I think my voice is cracking. "That...that you did that. How am I supposed to forgive you now?"

"I don't know!" he almost-yells. "I don't know. I was so...so blindsided. When you started dating her. I'd just been waiting for you to figure it out, for you to want me. And instead of me, you wanted her, and I'm a selfish shit stain, but I tried to be happy for you until you weren't happy anymore, and then I was just pissed. Because if I couldn't have you, at least you could have someone who was amazing to you and for you, and she *wasn't*, and it wasn't fucking fair."

I watch him there, looking so incredibly pathetic: eyes blurry like a hangover, dirty-brown roots showing along his part, crying and beyond upset and...it's stupid. That he's feeling that. Because I'm feeling that. That empty-achy-incurable throb. I know exactly how he feels.

His head is lowered now, trying to pull himself together, his hands clench each other. They are slender, white-knuckled Dagen fingers, writhing helplessly into each other, and it's so stupid. So I put my hands on top of them. Hold his balled fists in mine.

He looks up. Cheeks wet, eyes confused and hopeless. "How..."

"Dagen..."

"I'm sorry, Benji. I'm so fucking sorry." And it's like there's nothing left to say.

I bring his hands curiously to my mouth. He's got hangnails because he's stressed. I touch my lips to his cuticles, and his breathing stills.

"What...?"

"It...it was a long time ago," I say. I know it's feeble, that I should be giving myself real justification. "We were only seventeen."

"You can't," he whispers, and I think he means forgive him, but I can. I don't know why, but I have to.

"I can." I shrug. "There's nothing else I can do."

"What do you mean?" he asks, voice hoarse.

"I don't know. I don't fucking know." We pause. "I'm not happy without you," I say, finally. "I tried, and I can live just fine, better even, but I'm not happy. And you're not happy. And it's stupid. It's just stupid for us to both just sit around being unhappy."

"Benji... I don't know why you're doing this, but if you're serious, I'll do anything..."

"Tell me you felt miserable." I need him to get that I mean not because of what he's done.

His eyes widen slightly, and he licks his lips. Answers half-awed, like I've asked him the easiest thing in the world.

"I did. Goddamn. I feel so fucking miserable without you."

"Okay," I say.

His breath catches. "Okay?" he asks, so cautiously.

"Yeah. Okay."

He bites his lip, and when he lets it go he's smiling. Eyes wet, cheeks stained, and grinning uncontrollably.

"You're serious?"

"I'm serious. But also realize that I can, and will, bring this up each and every time we're in an argument," I joke.

"You'll never lose again," he promises.

"I never lost to begin with." I grin.

He sobers immediately. "So, you really mean it? That we can... try?"

I nod. "But slow. We're going slow. Because you fucking hurt me, Dagen."

He leans in over the table, and I meet him there. His lips hesitantly reach mine.

"You know," I say, as we break apart, barely an inch between us, "you could've just told me you loved me a long time ago, before Lillian, and we wouldn't've had to deal with all of this."

"I couldn't." He blushes, skin heating mine.

"You couldn't," I say, disbelief thick in my voice. "Don't be ridiculous, I know you've never cared about what people think about you."

"I don't care what people think about me. Just...person. Just you."

"You're a fuckhead."

"You've saved my life," he whispers, eyes closed. My hands cup his face and I keep him close. And...it's not perfect, and everything is not quite alright.

But it's fucking good enough.

Chapter Nineteen

I'M HUNGRY. FOR the first time in days. Resolving all these dramatics, I guess. So I finally lean away from Dagen's face. And stand. Go to the cupboard.

I'm reaching when Dagen's arms wrap around me from behind. He's quiet, and I'm concentrating, so I don't notice and I jump, startled.

"Not quite the reaction I was going for," he says.

"Learn to walk louder," I retort.

He nuzzles my neck, sending shivers down my spine and everything. Kisses my ear.

"So, this is really it? You'll keep me? I don't have to make amends, sweep the floor, sell my liver or anything?"

"Look around you, you moron. Does it look like there is anything left to clean in this bloody apartment? Being away from you inspires some pretty drastic reactions. And ew, I'm not a necrophiliac. Keep the liver."

"My very own obsessive compulsive," he whispers.

I whip around in his arms, so I'm facing him.

"I changed my mind," I say.

"What?"

"You have to go grocery shopping. Stock up, since you're moving back in. And I know about the key you had made. So you don't have to worry about lying about that. So. Groceries. I'm completely out of cereal."

He laughs at me. And I kiss him.

***

Once he's gone, I take a deep breath, still kind of shaky. Pick up the phone and dial.

"Benjamin?" Lillian's surprised, understandably, as I've been avoiding her for how many weeks now?

"Uh, yeah."

"I didn't think you'd actually call," she admits.

"Well...I can hang up and pretend I didn't, if you want..."

"What?" She's freaked, I can tell. I can see her, blithering around her little apartment. "No! That's not...what...I mean. Hi."

"Hi."

"Are you... Is everything..."

"Everything is shitty. But, we're pushing past it."

"What?"

"I'm miserable without him, and I need a friend to talk to, now that my best friend is my boyfriend, so... So I'm letting it go. And it's not fair to just forgive one of you...so...this is your... forgiveness phone call."

"Really?"

"Really."

"Oh." Her voice is quiet, and for a moment, I mistake her silence for a total lack of enthusiasm—until I hear her sniff. Oh, fuck. Tears. What a great way to rekindle a friendship.

"You alright?" I ask.

"No. I mean, yes. More than alright. Are you sure you want to, because I can understand if you want to like, enact violence upon my person or..."

"Meh, it's alright, I'll go with sleeping with your boyfriend."

A shocked little silence.

"It's a joke, Lillian. Remember? You're usually so good at those..."

She's crying again, and laughing, and it just feels right to have everything back in place again.

"You know I'm sorry, right?" she whispers. "That I should've told you. It's the stupidest thing I've ever done, and I hated myself for it...still do...and—"

"Lils. We're all stupid sometimes."

"...Okay."

"I'll call you this week?"

"Yeah?" The little note of hopefulness in her voice is contagious.

"Okay."

"Benjamin?"

"Yeah?"

"I really do love you, okay?"

"I know. It's fine. We'll be fine."

"Okay."

"And Lils?"

"Yeah?"

"I love you, too. I'm fucking mad at you, but I love you."

"Thanks. Thanks, Ben. That means a lot."

***

One year later

We're backstage. First show of the new tour, and I'm a little jumpy. Dagen's behind me, keeps kissing the back of my neck.

"Fuck off!" I tell him, but he doesn't listen. Just lowers his mouth, skimming lips over my scar, his mark, on my shoulder.

I'm trying to go through the set list in my head. Not that I'll forget it; we've gone over it a million times. I'm just nervous. And he's so fucking annoying.

"Dagen! Piss off!"

"On in one," someone directs.

Dagen's grin expands, we've waited too long between shows for his liking.

"Kiss," he demands.

I roll my eyes but kiss him, wondering if I should be used to him, numbed to the way we are together, but I'm not. Not ever. He races a track over the roof of my mouth, uncaring of who's around.

"Play a good show, Benji," he whispers finally.

***

"This is a song," Dagen starts, between songs, "for someone…" he walks seductively towards me. I hold my guitar up as a buffer, and Doug produces that threatening little sound on his bass. Dagen slips his hand over my skin, causing the girls to fucking scream. And I'm kind of uncomfortable, because I've never been one for PDA and I know I show it, what, with his hand hot on my hipbone, looking right into my eyes, making me blush. The girls scream even louder.

"…that won't leave your thoughts alone…and all you want to do…" He brings his mouth towards my neck.

I see him there. And this is it. It's my move. Threading one hand in his hair, I yank him upwards, away from my neck. For one half of a second, our eyes stay connected, and I see the grin there, and the moment seems to go on for fucking ever, but I know it's just a second. Less than a second. I bring him close, my guitar hanging at my neck by the strap, untouched by me as I pull him inwards, lips colliding, mouths pulsing together. And everything's all screaming and bright lights, and noise and noise and noise.

But mostly
it's Dagen.

THE END

About the Author

Anne O'Gleadra is currently taking the most circuitous route through academia known to humanity. Thankfully, she gets to do so on majestic Vancouver Island, where she spends her time procrastinating, devouring podcasts, and telling her cat how cute she is. She is perpetually grateful to her extraordinarily kind friends and indulgent family whose support means just about everything.

By the Author

It's Like This

Meaning It

Beaten Track Publishing

For more titles from Beaten Track Publishing,
please visit our website:

http://www.beatentrackpublishing.com

Thanks for reading!